Perchance of Death

The city is of Night; perchance of Death,
But certainly of Night.
                    —James Thomson
                    The City of Dreadful Night

Swarming city, city full of dreams, where a ghost
in daylight clutches a passer-by! Mysteries everywhere
flow like sap in the narrow channels of the great giant.
                    —Charles Baudelaire
                    Les Sept Vieillards

As Elizabeth Linington:

PERCHANCE OF DEATH
CRIME BY CHANCE
PRACTISE TO DECEIVE
POLICEMAN'S LOT
SOMETHING WRONG
NO EVIL ANGEL

DATE WITH DEATH
GREENMASK
THE KINGBREAKER
MONSIEUR JANVIER
THE LONG WATCH
THE PROUD MAN

As Egan O'Neill:

THE ANGLOPHILE

As Lesley Egan:

THE BLIND SEARCH
SCENES OF CRIME
PAPER CHASE
MALICIOUS MISCHIEF
IN THE DEATH OF A MAN
THE WINE OF VIOLENCE
A SERIOUS INVESTIGATION
THE NAMELESS ONES

SOME AVENGER, RISE
DETECTIVE'S DUE
MY NAME IS DEATH
RUN TO EVIL
AGAINST THE EVIDENCE
THE BORROWED ALIBI
A CASE FOR APPEAL

As Dell Shannon:

STREETS OF DEATH
DEUCES WILD
CRIME FILE
SPRING OF VIOLENCE
NO HOLIDAY FOR CRIME
WITH INTENT TO KILL
MURDER WITH LOVE

THE RINGER
WHIM TO KILL
UNEXPECTED DEATH
CRIME ON THEIR HANDS
SCHOOLED TO KILL
KILL WITH KINDNESS
CHANCE TO KILL

iv

RAIN WITH VIOLENCE   DOUBLE BLUFF
WITH A VENGEANCE   DEATH OF A BUSYBODY
COFFIN CORNER   KNAVE OF HEARTS
DEATH BY INCHES   EXTRA KILL
THE DEATH BRINGERS   THE ACE OF SPADES
MARK OF MURDER   CASE PENDING
ROOT OF ALL EVIL

Perchance of Death

ELIZABETH LININGTON

PUBLISHED FOR THE CRIME CLUB BY
DOUBLEDAY & COMPANY, INC.
GARDEN CITY, NEW YORK
1977

All of the characters in this book
are fictitious, and any resemblance
to actual persons, living or dead,
is purely coincidental.

Library of Congress Cataloging in Publication Data

Linington, Elizabeth.
Perchance of death.

I. Title.
PZ4.L756Pe   [PS3562.I515]   813'.5'4
ISBN: 0-385-13081-3
Library of Congress Catalog Card Number 76–52221

First Edition

For Elaine, who liked it

Perchance of Death

CHAPTER 1

Detective-Sergeant and Policewoman Maddox climbed the creaking stairs of the old Wilcox Street (Hollywood) precinct station in silence. On the landing, Sue said, "It's not fair."

"As an experienced cop, you expect life to be fair?" said Maddox. "If at first you don't succeed—"

Sue gave him a withering look and turned right into the small office she shared with Sergeant Daisy Hoffman. Daisy was there, just uncovering her typewriter. "It isn't fair, you know," said Sue.

"Oh? No luck again, I take it," said Daisy, cocking her neat blond head.

"When you think," said Sue, "of all the unwed mothers, and hordes of illegitimate children just to get the welfare money, not to speak of all these obscene abortions—and one respectable upright couple who want a family can't seem to get started." She hung up her raincoat and sat down at her desk.

"The doctor—"

"Don't tell me what the doctor says. There's no reason I shouldn't get pregnant, just relax and don't worry about it. Which is what Mother says too."

"Excellent advice," said Daisy, who was an experienced grandmother.

"It's all very well for you to talk," said Sue crossly.

"That's a good-looking dress—new?" asked Daisy diplomatically.

"On sale." Having passed the detectives' exam, Sue was no longer required to wear a uniform. "And the weather's gone crazy, I think. Rain again, in September—the first time in sixty-nine years, the paper said. Have we got anything new?"

"Another burglary, possibly tied up to that one last week.

And Juanita was out again last night—I can hear the boys cussing."

"Give them some work to do for a change," said Sue. The phone rang, she picked it up and said, "Yes, J—" and caught herself. Their erstwhile desk sergeant, Johnny O'Neill, had finally passed his physical after more surgery and departed happily for a squad car and street action again. His replacement had been on the desk only this week, a taciturn middle-aged man from downtown named Whitwell. "Yes?" said Sue.

"Some citizens with a missing report. Maybe not just the usual—you'd better hear about it. Mr. and Mrs. Strange, Mrs. Nichols."

"Send them up," said Sue resignedly. The rain was drumming furiously against the one window, and the stark single fluorescent lamp made the small office in this shabby, ancient building look shabbier than ever, with its scarred golden-oak desks and chairs, the one old file cabinet for current paper work. Taxpayers who visited this precinct might conceivably wonder where their money went, except that they were usually preoccupied with other worries.

The trio who arrived on the landing a minute later didn't look much interested in their surroundings. Sue said, "Mr. and Mrs. Strange? Would you like to come in here, please? I'm Mrs. Maddox—Sergeant Hoffman."

The older couple was in their forties, ordinary-looking solid citizens. He was tall and spare, balding, in a rumpled gray suit, tie askew, an ancient trench coat; she was a little plump, dark-haired, round-faced, a trifle dowdy in black dress and sturdy cotton stockings. The young woman behind them was in the early twenties, if that, pretty and blond in a navy pantsuit. Daisy offered chairs and they sat down. Mrs. Strange struggled out of her beige raincoat and let it crumple over the back of the chair. They all looked at the policewomen with something like indignant bewilderment, a look familiar to Sue and Daisy from the citizens new to any police station.

"We just can't think what happened to her," said Mrs. Strange. "She wouldn't have just gone off somewhere like that —some of these girls, the things you hear, the things that happen, but Pauline's not like that—and we called Bill right off but he was staying over with a friend, his mother said—he wouldn't know anything—"

"Now, Mother. We'd better tell it in order." He patted her shoulder. Three pairs of eyes held the same anxiety, but the younger woman looked faintly curious too, at the office, at Sue and Daisy. "It's our younger daughter, Pauline, we don't know where she's gone, she never left a note or—"

"And she never said a word to me, and she would have. Oh, I'm her sister, I ought to—"

"Mrs. Nichols."

"That's right. I won't say we never had any differences, but we're pretty close—I'm only two years older. Pauline's nearly eighteen—"

"And she's a good girl," said Mrs. Strange. "Not wild like some young people—a good sensible girl, last year in high and pretty good marks, and"—she gave a sudden wail—"what could have *happened*—she just wasn't *there* when we got home last night—you tell them, Sylvia—"

"And she should have been," said her sister. "Now don't take on, Mama, that doesn't do any good. You see, she'd been out with Bob and me. We've just joined this square-dancing club, old-fashioned dancing, see, and she said she'd like to go, see what it was like. So we picked her up at home about seven last night. Dad and Mama were going out for dinner—"

"To the Ballisters'," put in her mother irrelevantly, "just a quiet evening—old friends—but we got to playing five hundred and it was late when we got home, way after midnight—"

"We dropped Pauline off at the house a little after eleven," said Sylvia Nichols. "She had her own key, of course. She was on the porch when we drove off—as far as I knew she was just going in to bed."

"And she wasn't there when we got home," said Strange. "So we called Sylvia, naturally, and when she said—"

"Are any of her clothes missing?" asked Daisy. "I take it there wasn't any sign in the house as if she'd been attacked, or hurt, or you'd have called in then."

They blanched; that was a new idea. "No—no, of course not," said Strange. "The doors were all locked just as usual. But no sign of her, and Pauline wouldn't just go off—"

"I think all her things are there," said Mrs. Strange. "She never meant to go anywhere, she left her homework all spread out on her desk for over the weekend—"

"And we couldn't get hold of Bill—like we said—he's her boy friend, only fellow she's ever dated, a nice young fellow, Bill Blackwell—he'll be in class now, I guess, he goes to L.A.C.C. But we got hold of Alice, Alice Goodman, that's Pauline's best girl friend, and she didn't know anything at all." Strange shook his head. "We just can't imagine—"

Sue looked at Daisy with raised brows. It might be something; it might be nothing. The girl was eighteen; all this sounded as if she was a fairly responsible girl, but more background might tell a different story. "You'd better give us a description," said Daisy. Check the hospitals. Mundane things happened; she could have decided to visit the nearest pizza parlor and been knocked down by a drunk driver.

"Yes, sure, Pauline's five-five, about a hundred and twenty pounds, I think—dark brown hair, hazel eyes—"

"She had on a coral pantsuit and a white raincoat," said Sylvia, "and black loafers and she had a black purse, kind of a little velvet clutch."

Daisy made quick notes. They'd check the hospitals first, see if anything showed.

Across the hall in the big communal detectives' office, Maddox was reading the night-watch report and swearing about it to D'Arcy and Feinman. It was Friday, so Rodriguez was off. Rowan was typing a report; Dabney wasn't in yet, nor George Ellis. "I swear to God," said Maddox, "if it wasn't for females, this damn job wouldn't be such a headache. What the hell we're supposed to do with this I'd like to know. Juanita!"

"I saw it," said D'Arcy with a yawn. His lank seventy-six inches were draped lazily in the desk chair; he was desultorily looking through yesterday's *Herald-Examiner*. "Nothing much we can do with it. Another ride on the merry-go-round."

Maddox reread Dick Brougham's report with annoyance. Over the last four months, twelve men had come in with complaints against Juanita, and it was in the cards she had taken other marks who hadn't complained, feeling like idiots. Juanita was described in much the same terms by all of them—five feet to five-one, a hundred pounds or so, good figure, but the typed descriptions were hardly as graphic as those offered in person. "Brother, but stacked!" was the comment of Dennis Weaver, number one, echoed by all the rest up to William Rutherford last night. "A real cutie-pie, and dressed real cute, too, kind of far out but cute—real short dress, bright red, and a fur coat some kind, she's got a swell pair of gams—kind of Mex-looking, maybe a touch o' the tarbrush, too, she's real dark, but brother, stacked! And I mean, it was such a hell of a surprise—I never thought she was no farmer's daughter, but I wasn't expecting a gun, for God's sake—"

Juanita was a very accommodating girl who quietly picked up the johns in bars—all good-class bars so far, and to date twelve different ones. The johns, all men in well-paying jobs and looking it, weren't hard to pick up, not for Juanita. But with the price arranged, they followed her out to the street, to a parking lot, to a parked car, to find Juanita poking a gun in their ribs. She had taken a respectable haul so far: fifty-eight dollars, an expensive watch, and a diamond ring from Weaver, a hundred and twenty dollars, a watch, and platinum wedding ring from Rutherford, and similar loot from the other ten in between. There was no way to track her down, short of putting a plainclothes detective on watch around the clock in every middle-class bar in Hollywood, which was impractical. The bartenders didn't know her, or the cashiers, or the regular clientele. They would go on asking, just in case; another tedious job and probably nothing to show for it.

Except for Juanita, it had been a fairly slow night: a hit-run on Sunset, a heist at a liquor store on Van Ness, a knifing in a bar brawl, one D.O.A. At least that didn't look like making much work: the body had been found on the sidewalk along Sunset Boulevard by Patrolman Carmichael, and was probably another old wino succumbing to a heart attack or whatever; no I.D., but the prints might be in their files. Somebody had better go to the morgue to get his prints. Maddox said as much, and Feinman said, "That's where Dabney is. You were late. He said he might go on to that liquor store, the owner didn't think the heister touched anything but you never know, and Dabney likes to be thorough."

"Thorough!" said Maddox. "Can you quote the statistics

offhand, just how often we pick up good enough latents, prints that happen to be on file, to make a case?"

"Not very often," said Feinman mildly, "I know."

The rain beat on the windows and D'Arcy folded over a page of his newspaper. "Did you know this is the first time it's rained in September since 1907? Funny." A mutter of thunder sounded in the distance. Nobody commented.

The phone rang on Maddox' desk and he picked it up. "Wilcox Street Police Station, Sergeant Maddox."

"This is Dr. Hirschner at Hollywood Receiving." The voice was young, but sounded tired and faintly cynical. "You'll be interested to know that we've got another battered child. Just as of now. Not much on it yet but enough to identify her."

"Oh, fine," said Maddox. "You've got a name—parents' address?"

"Both. You'll be getting a formal report," said Hirschner. "The child's dead. Ten minutes ago."

"God," said Maddox. "We'd better come up and hear about it." He put the phone down, got up, and prodded D'Arcy. "Come on, we've got work to do."

They got into their raincoats again; downstairs in the lobby they met Dabney coming in. "I got the drunk's prints, but not a hope in hell at that liquor store—just a lot of smudges."

"As per usual," said Maddox. It was raining steadily, a hard downpour. D'Arcy folded himself into the passenger seat of Maddox' little blue Maserati unprotestingly for the short ride.

Six blocks up Wilcox Street they ducked out of the car, across a flooding parking lot into the solid block of the big hospital, and were directed to Emergency, where they found Hirschner. He was a fair, rather handsome youngish man nearly as tall as D'Arcy, with shrewd pale blue eyes. "You'd better have a look," he said. Neither of them particularly wanted to, but that was part of the job too; they followed him down to a room at the end of the corridor, hardly more than a closet, where a very small form lay still under a sheet on a narrow cot. "I'll send her down to the morgue now—you'll want a full autopsy." He pulled back the sheet.

"Christ," said D'Arcy. "People." The child couldn't be more than three, and you couldn't tell if she'd been pretty or not, the face was too swollen and darkened with bruises. There were more bruises all over the little body, and what looked like partly healed abrasions. Hirschner lifted the body and turned it over, and D'Arcy said "Christ" again.

"Burns," said Hirschner. "My guess would be somebody held live cigarettes on her. And it's been going on some time —some of these marks are a month or so old."

Maddox had his notebook out. "So what else can you tell us?"

Hirschner straightened, put back the sheet, and led the way out to the corridor. "She was brought in about forty-five minutes ago by a man. I can't tell you his name. He said she'd fallen downstairs and her mother had to go to work, asked him to bring her in. The nurse got the mother's name—a Mrs. Candy Thomas, address on DeLongpre. The child was comatose then and there wasn't much red tape—the nurse called me and we got her into a treatment room. I started oxygen but she died about ten minutes later." He shrugged. "Possibly a fractured skull, internal bleeding—the autopsy will say. But you can see she's been subjected to brutal treatment over a long time."

"Yes. Have you tried to contact the mother? Talk to the man?"

"When I came out he was gone. Just walked out when the nurse tried to get more information out of him. I haven't called the mother."

"Leaving the dirty work to us," said D'Arcy. "Don't tell me, it's our job."

"Well, it'll add up to manslaughter at the least," said Hirschner.

They went down the hall to talk to the nurse at the admitting Emergency desk; she was a slim, dark young woman with alert eyes. "I know, Dr. Hirschner told me," she said to Maddox' badge; her voice was distressed. "A terrible thing—the kind of thing hard to believe, but you wouldn't believe how often we do see it—"

"Yes, we would. We're cops," said Maddox. And even as he questioned her, made a few notes, he noticed irrelevantly that he was having the usual effect on anything female: she smoothed her neat dark head and her eyes were interested, aware. He would never understand it; thin, dark Ivor Maddox, who had just slid in to the force at five-nine, was a very unremarkable fellow; it was just peculiar about the females, and a good thing Sue wasn't given to jealousy.

"He didn't say much. He told me the mother's name"—she pushed over a memo sheet—"and I could see she needed immediate attention, I called the doctor, and he took her right into treatment. Usually we get more details before, but— Then I tried to get more information, it's just routine, about any medical insurance, which firm, policy number, if it's on-the-job insurance covering any minors—you know—"

"All the red tape," said Maddox, "wound around us these socialistic days. And?"

"He just kept saying he didn't know, we'd have to ask the mother. He wouldn't give me his name, just said he was 'a friend of the kid's old lady.' And that she'd come to get the kid after work and pay us then. Well, you know, it's customary to ask for a deposit if there's no insurance—"

"Yes," said Maddox, and she flared up in momentary resentment, quick to suspect the nuance.

"You needn't think—I mean, sometimes people seem to think we're just grabbing for the money before we treat the patient—I saw the child was in a bad way, I called the doctor at once, but it is customary—after all we're not running a charity here—"

"All right," said Maddox. "What did he say when you told him that?"

"He just looked surprised and then he said he didn't have any money on him. He said he'd call the mother, I'd told him we'd have to have her permission anyway for anything but strictly emergency treatment—and I assumed he was heading for the public phones down the hall, but when the doctor came out he was just gone, we couldn't find him any place."

"Can you tell us what he looked like?"

"Oh—I'm not very good at describing people. He was taller than you, maybe six feet—late twenties, I guess—sort of sandy hair, pretty long—scraggly, you know, down past his ears—and he looked sort of shabby, I mean he had on old gray slacks and a brown sweater and a dirty raincoat—but that might not mean anything, I suppose, because people do put on old clothes to go out in the rain, in California anyway.

It's one thing I noticed right away when I came out here from New York, I suppose it's because it doesn't rain often here and people haven't got the right clothes for it."

"Thanks very much," said Maddox.

"I hope you find him—and whoever hurt that poor child."

"So do we."

They got back in the Maserati and drove out to the address on DeLongpre. It was one side of a narrow old duplex, a ramshackle frame house on that shabby, narrow old street. They got no answer from the one side, but the second door was opened by a tousled-looking young woman in a frayed chenille bathrobe.

"Sure I know Candy," she said through a yawn, and stared at the badges. "You're *cops?* What you want with Candy, for God's sake?"

"Do you know where she works? Her husband?"

"She hasn't got a husband, she's divorced. Yeah, she works at a Woolworth's, the one out on Santa Monica past Fairfax. What you guys want with Candy, anyway?"

Maddox thanked her. They'd probably be talking to her again. They found a parking slot a block away from the Woolworth store and sloshed back to it through the rain. Inside, they found the manager, who pointed out Mrs. Candy Thomas behind the cosmetic counter. Maddox hadn't showed the badge, and he was incurious, a busy man.

They both, however, showed the badges to Candy Thomas, who stared at them. She was a vapidly pretty blonde about twenty-five, with a buxom figure, shocking-pink lipstick and nail polish, and a reedy voice. "P-police?" she said thinly.

"We're sorry to tell you that your daughter is dead," said Maddox deliberately.

She gave a loud gasp and then burst into noisy tears. "My little Peggy? Oh, dear God, poor Peggy—I didn't think she was hurt that bad, I didn't really—she just fell down the stairs—"

"Which stairs?" asked D'Arcy. "There aren't any where you live."

"Where—uh—where my girl friend lives. Oh, my poor little Peggy—"

Maddox and D'Arcy felt tired. They'd have to talk to her at

length, and probably a number of other people, on this one. She was attracting some attention from customers; they'd better adjourn elsewhere. They asked, and she had a car; D'Arcy took her out to it and rode back to the station with her while Maddox had another word with the manager and drove back alone. There, she sat in a chair between their desks and sobbed into a handkerchief and said they were mean to ask her questions when she'd just lost her own darling little girl.

"Who was battered to death," said D'Arcy. "You knew she was hurt badly enough to need a doctor, but you couldn't be bothered to take her yourself. Who did take her to the hospital?"

The one eye peering at him from the handkerchief looked a little wary. "I didn't think—well, it was Rex. My boy friend Rex, he works nights so he could take her."

"Rex who?"

"Slaney. Nobody did anything to Peggy—she fell down, was all."

"I'm afraid not, Mrs. Thomas," said Maddox. "What's his address?"

The rain poured down steadily. Across the room Dabney was on the phone. Feinman was typing a report. Sergeant Ellis came out of the lieutenant's office looking disgruntled and sat down at his desk to stare into space.

Beyond the open door Maddox saw Sue and Daisy coming back from somewhere, shedding dripping coats as they went into the office across the hall.

"All right, Mrs. Thomas. Did you ever punish Peggy? How? What for?"

"I never spanked her. Nobody hurt Peggy. You dumb cops, always picking on people— I told you, she fell downstairs."

"I don't know, Sue," said Daisy, wrinkling her nose at the typewriter. "It's a funny setup. It could be something serious. It's just funny enough."

"And at the same time, no real handle to it," said Sue. "Nothing happened in that house. They're all obviously concerned about her, not covering up anything. And Mrs. Strange is what Mother calls a nasty-nice housekeeper. Everything neat as a pin, the girl's room just a little untidy in a natural way, and her apologizing as if it was a pigsty. And they're careful people—dead-bolt locks and a double lock on the back door."

"Mmh, yes," said Daisy. "Nobody ambushed the girl in the house. And the sister says she was on the front porch, where the light was on, unlocking the door, the last glimpse she had."

They thought about it. They knew now that Pauline Strange wasn't in any hospital nearby as an accident victim.

"There's the simplest explanation," said Daisy. "The boy friend. The only one she ever had. We haven't looked for him yet. So maybe they decided to drive over to Vegas and get married."

"Starting at midnight, in the pouring rain? And her mother says none of her clothes are missing."

"Yes, I know," said Daisy. "It's funny."

There was still paper work to do, people to see, on the latest burglary. They had helped the boys out before, hunting for Juanita, and might get roped in on that again. There was the usual list of runaways, but not much any cops anywhere could do about that. Sometime in the next week or so Daisy would be spending an unspecified length of time in court testifying at a narco trial. And doubtless there would be new things coming up from day to day.

"I've just got time to do this report before lunch," said Sue. "You can start looking for the boy friend. Said to be going to L.A.C.C."

Feinman looked into the office diffidently. "Can I borrow one of you for a while?"

"What for?" asked Daisy.

"We've just had a make on that D.O.A. Seems he wasn't a drunk derelict after all. Perfectly respectable fellow, night security guard at United Artists Studio. Looks as if he had a heart attack or something on the way to his car maybe. They made him from his prints, he had a navy record. Anyway, we just had word from downtown, his wife's reported him missing, and I thought one of you could come along to break the news."

"Oh, all right." Sue got up and reached for her coat.

"It's all the way down to Manhattan Beach," said Feinman.

"Well, for heaven's sake drive carefully," said Daisy. "I expect the farmers need it but personally I've had enough rain."

"The funny thing is," Feinman said seriously on the way downstairs, "the farmers are mad as hell about it, the papers say. It's too soon and ruining all sorts of crops."

"Which I suppose is going to send prices up again."

"And the paper this morning said no letup in sight."

"You're just a ray of sunshine," said Sue.

The usual routine of the office, always unfinished business to be cleared away, made the schedule a little tight. There were two citizens coming in to make formal statements on the new burglary and the one last Tuesday night. Ellis and Rowan had an appointment with a deputy D.A. in regard to the upcoming trial of a narco peddler, and that left them shorthanded. Before Maddox and D'Arcy had finished a preliminary questioning of Candy Thomas, word came in that the hit-run victim of last night had regained consciousness; someone would have to talk to her.

They hadn't got much out of Candy at this first session but the boy friend's name. They wanted to talk to him, and to some of their friends, and the neighbors, but it didn't look as if they'd get much of that done today. She'd given them an address for Rex Slaney, an apartment on Leland Way a block over from DeLongpre. D'Arcy went to have a look there while Maddox went over to the hospital.

The hit-run victim was Mrs. Cora Appin, and she looked at Maddox apologetically, propped up in the hospital bed. "Giving the police all this trouble," she said. "I feel ashamed." She was a sprightly-looking old lady, wiry and white-haired. She had a broken leg and a slight concussion, but she had all her wits about her and gave Maddox a bright smile, trying to sit up straighter. "Oh, this is my daughter Amy. As soon as I came to myself I told the nurse for goodness' sake to call her, she'd be wild finding me not there this morning—"

The daughter, who was a carbon copy of her mother, only a

little less wiry and wrinkled, laughed a jolly laugh. "The silly thing is, I wasn't!" she told Maddox. "I never knew a thing about it. I was just getting into bed when Mother said she was going down to the corner for a hamburger—Pete's open till midnight—and I never knew she hadn't come home. Mother's a night owl and I'm not, you see, when I got up her door was shut and naturally I didn't disturb her, and off I went to work with never a worry in my mind—you could've knocked me over with a feather when Mr. Unkovich called me in and said the hospital wanted me!"

"And all my own fault," said Mrs. Appin. "I feel ashamed, acting like an old fool."

"No reason to feel that way," said Maddox. "You know we'd like to find out who hit you and didn't stop. Can you tell me anything about the car?"

"Not much. It was a little car, like one of these foreign ones, only now the American factories make little ones too. Well, I do feel it was my own fault. Silly old fool, go barging out in the rain like that—I know well enough you're supposed to be careful, wear light-colored clothes and all, carry a flashlight—but heavens to Betsy, I know the neighborhood so good, living there forty years, I just never thought. Slipped on my old black coat and stuck my change purse in my pocket and off I went. I don't suppose that driver could've seen me till he was right on me, there isn't a light at that corner anyway, just a crosswalk. And by the same token I never saw him till the last minute, I think he'd just come around the corner of Mansfield there. Well, a-course he should've stopped, but I guess it was half my fault anyway, and he might've thought it was a dog or something—"

Maddox didn't offer the opinion that it came to the same thing: a life. Thinking about little Peggy Thomas, just short of three years old. And he was reminded of Sue's fulminations over those dog poisonings two months ago: "Anybody who'd poison a dog would do the same to a child"—which was only cold logic. What it came down to was simple lack of empathy —dogs, children, or old ladies.

Once in a while, busman's holiday, he picked up a copy of *True Detective, Official Detective;* and one factor in some of those stories had struck him: the difference in reaction to crime between city and country. There wasn't much difference in the criminals; but out in the rural fastnesses where people were few and far between, there seemed to be a little more caring about people, more co-operation. In the city, any city, with neighbors unknown, homes temporary, crowds faceless, there was a singular lack of brothers' keepers around.

At any rate, Mrs. Appin couldn't help them on the hit-run car; that would be filed away as unsolvable, and possibly the guilty one's conscience would bother him some but Maddox wouldn't gamble on it.

He had a belated lunch at the Grotto on Santa Monica; no one else from the station was there. It was still pouring. When he got back to the office at three o'clock D'Arcy was just in, dripping. He said, "No luck. Slaney wasn't home. I talked to the neighbors, but they don't know him."

"So we're back to what Candy told us." She had said, sullenly, that Rex played sax in a combo, jobs at a couple of places, a disco on the Strip, a restaurant with a floor show in Westwood.

"Yep. I tried both places. Both closed, but the managers were there. They don't know much about the combo—it's officially led by one Barney Yates—booked as Barney's Boys. They didn't even know where any of them live, why should they? But I suppose he'll show up on the job, or at home, sometime."

"I suppose," said Maddox. "People are stupid that way." He rubbed the back of his neck. Picking up the cigarette pack from his desk, he discovered it was empty and went out to the machine in the hall. When he looked into the office across the way, he found his better half crouched over her typewriter busy on a report, one eye screwed up against smoke from the cigarette in one corner of her mouth. "The modern woman," he said. "You look like the original Girl Friday in whatever that old movie was."

Sue removed the cigarette and sat up straight. "Ivor Goronwy Maddox, if you so much as mention those obnoxious Libbers to me—all these damnable abortions—and that poor soul just went to pieces, a nice woman and he was only fifty-four—and this missing report all up in the air, nothing to it really but it could be something—and all the damned paper work on this burglary—"

"We are being put upon," said Maddox. "It's a thankless job, love."

"And wandering around in all this rain—I'm a mess, I'll have to do my hair all over again tonight—"

"You look reasonably attractive to me," said Maddox, surveying her slightly disheveled dark brown coiffure, "if your nose does need powdering and you've chewed off your lipstick. I've got to go out on some overtime tonight."

"Oh? What on?"

"We have a battered child. Dead. Girl, three years old. I want to talk to the mother's boy friend, and he plays sax in a combo."

"That, of course, is all I needed to make my day. Honestly, Ivor! Honestly, how do human people get this way? And why are we such damned fools as to try to cope with them?"

"Same answer," said Maddox. " 'Man He made a little lower than the angels.' I'll take you out to dinner."

"We shouldn't, at restaurant prices now, but—O.K.," said Sue. "With a drink first. I'll need one by then."

"Deal," said Maddox, and got his cigarettes and went back to his desk. "So we do some overtime to find Slaney. Where's he supposed to be playing tonight?"

"The Shamrock Inn, Westwood," said D'Arcy. "O.K. with me." He was a bachelor.

"No date?" Maddox eyed him interestedly. D'Arcy was extremely susceptible to falling into precipitate love; but since he'd broken off with his latest flame a good six months ago, he'd apparently been treading the straight and narrow path.

He just said a little morosely, "Meet you here at eight."

"O.K.," said Maddox, and his phone rang. This time it was the desk.

"You've got a homicide," said Sergeant Whitwell genially. "Squad car just called in. It's Poinsettia Street, Gomez is there preserving the scene."

"Thank you so much," said Maddox.

They took D'Arcy's Dodge. It was a neat, newly painted frame bungalow behind two patches of green lawn with a cement walk up to the porch. Patrolman Gomez was on the front porch with an excited boy about thirteen.

"After I took a look through the window I just called in, Sergeant," said Gomez. "The back door's been forced—I didn't touch it."

"Gee!" said the boy. "Gee, will I have a story to tell! Old Mis' Peller getting murdered! Gee!"

"This is Ron Keller," said Gomez. "He's the one called."

"I sure did!" said the boy. "See, she was always real good about paying, first time I'd come, see. See, I deliver the *Herald-Examiner* this route, and some people, it's a real pain, they say come back on Tuesday and like that—the Ponds down the next block, sometimes I got to go back four–five times—but old Mis' Peller was always real good about it. And she hardly ever went any place, I mean she was always home evenings, see. So I was surprised I couldn't raise her last night, it was about seven, I guess, I went out after supper to collect. So I figured try her again this afternoon, after school. And I rang and rang, and then I was so surprised, see, I just looked in the front window. Gee! Gee! You can see the blood —and things all in a mess—and her right there! So I went up to the corner drugstore and called you."

Maddox and D'Arcy moved across the deep front porch and peered through the one wide window. Even on this dark day, sufficient light streamed in there from windows at the side that they could see a body sprawled on the living-room floor, dark streaks on face and arms, overturned furniture.

"Gee," said Ron Keller excitedly, "I bet somebody busted in and murdered her for all her money!"

"Did she have a lot of money?" asked D'Arcy.

"Oh, yessir, she sure did, everybody knew that! Her husband, he's dead now, but he sued some big company for about a million dollars, and she never spent nothing hardly, made out to be pretty poor, so must be she still had it."

Maddox raised his brows at D'Arcy. "So let's look at the back door."

"Anybody could've opened it with an old four-ward key," said Gomez. "But it looks even simpler—he just forced the lock and walked in."

CHAPTER 2

The flimsy screen on the back door had been wrenched off its hinges, which wouldn't have taken a Samson. The back door itself, with its inadequate lock, had just been forced in bodily. Leaving Gomez outside with the boy, Maddox and D'Arcy went into an old-fashioned square kitchen, very clean and neat. The rest of the place was in wild disorder: drawers pulled out and dumped in the two small bedrooms, clothes out of the closets in a heap on the floor; in the dining room, dishes had been swept from the built-in sideboard to broken chaos on the floor, those drawers emptied of a litter of table-cloths, other miscellany. In the small living room, lamps were smashed, tables overturned, and beside the little imitation hearth with its gas heater the old woman was sprawled in rigid death, one hand incongruously clutching a revolver, the blood dried and dark on her face and hands. She was a short, stout, dumpy old lady, wearing a knee-length, corduroy house robe.

"She put up a fight," said D'Arcy. "At a guess, by what the boy said, yesterday afternoon? Or morning—she wasn't dressed."

"Maybe she didn't intend to go out in the rain," said Maddox. The gun looked like a .22.

They didn't do much looking around; there might be a wealth of evidence here for the lab. They went out and called the station from the squad car; Rowan and Dabney came out with the mobile lab truck. They sent the boy on his way, and he went reluctantly, and Gomez went back on tour. Maddox and D'Arcy split up and went to talk to neighbors; an hour later they met back at the house to compare notes.

"Nobody heard anything, of course," said D'Arcy, "in all

this rain—doors and windows shut. Or saw anything. The woman on the east side was out shopping all afternoon anyway. Mrs. Peller had lived here at least thirty years, but nobody seemed to know her very well. I gather that some neighbors she used to know better have died or moved."

"Um," said Maddox. "About what I got. The kind of neighborhood that used to be permanent, settled, people knowing each other, but these days—" A number of modest houses similar to this one along this block, but where once they'd been occupied by owners, many would now be rented to the transients coming and going; and there were two new apartment buildings not far away. "The woman on the other side was home, watching TV. Everybody's concerned about it, what's the neighborhood coming to, but nobody said oh, poor old Mrs. Peller. I did hear the rumor again, she had a lot of money."

D'Arcy went over to where Dabney was dusting a little overturned table. "You doing any good, Bob?"

"Hell of a lot of latents, good and bad. Probably mostly hers. The morgue wagon ought to be here—we've got enough photographs. You can have the gun, I've dusted it. One slug fired and so far we haven't found it anywhere. By the way, the mailbox is full, so it probably happened yesterday."

"What we figured," agreed Maddox. If they got anything useful here it would be from the lab. It was getting on toward the end of shift then; they left Rowan and Dabney still at work, presently to seal the house and take off too, and went back to the station. D'Arcy said amiably he didn't mind writing the initial report; he'd go out for a hamburger or something.

Maddox and Sue drove separately up to Musso and Frank's and had a fairly quick drink before dinner. Sue asked about the new homicide, and Maddox said, "The more things change—it's depressing. I suppose the old girl could have had a fortune in diamonds stashed away, but it doesn't seem likely. She was old, lived alone, didn't go out of her way to be friendly, so the rumor went around she was a miser, of course. I'd take a bet X is somebody from around there, or who knew somebody around there. But in the middle of town—call it a thousand people who could have heard that. Wait and see what the lab turns up. And let's leave the office talk for the office."

"There's always the weather, of course. The five o'clock news said continued rain."

The place was crowded; they had to wait for their meal, and Maddox gulped a second cup of coffee, looking at his watch. "Damn it, it's nearly eight—I hope I won't be late, love, call it ten."

"Oh, I've got plenty to do," said Sue. "Wash my hair again, and a manicure." He saw her off in her old Chrysler, and drove back to the station to meet D'Arcy. They took the Dodge down to the Shamrock Inn, which was just inside Westwood but scarcely matched the classy address: a sleazy old stucco building on a corner of Wilshire, with a marquee silently screaming TOPLESS GIRLS!

Nobody there liked them very much, the manager or the girls or the combo. The combo was supposed to be there for an eight-thirty floor show, and they were all there but Rex Slaney. Barney Yates was annoyed about that, and even more annoyed at cops turning up and asking questions.

"No, I don't know where he is—I already tried his pad—and listen, he's a good sax man but I can get a dozen just as good any day, he don't want the damn job. And no, I don't know one damn thing about his girl friends or their damn kids, for God's sake, and listen, we got a show to do—good-bye."

None of the other three knew much about Slaney either; he'd joined the bunch only a month or so ago, when their regular sax man had a fight with Barney. Maddox and D'Arcy left the place without regret and, the evening being fairly young, headed back to Hollywood and DeLongpre Avenue.

Candy let them in unwillingly. "Cops pestering people. Just when I had such a terrible thing happen. I got some friends here—you might have the decency, leave me alone—"

The place was eloquent, now they saw the inside. Not Candy's fault that she couldn't afford a bright new apartment: this was vintage Hollywood, a cramped shabby cheap place, camped in by a fifty-year succession of tenants without much money. But it was all unclean, untidy, redolent of careless living without order or routine. The friends were a bonus: two couples about Candy's age, introduced reluctantly. Jim and Doris Hobson, Larry King, Gail Andrews. They eyed the cops nervously too.

Maddox flicked an eye at D'Arcy and said, "Maybe you wouldn't mind talking to Detective D'Arcy somewhere else— I've got just a few questions for Mrs. Thomas." D'Arcy shepherded them out to the kitchen and shut the door.

"Embarrass me in front of my friends—" She started to cry, sniffing into a handkerchief. "When my poor little girl—"

"Is dead of a series of brutal beatings," said Maddox. "By the way, we haven't heard anything about Peggy's father. You're divorced?"

"That's right. Just after she was born. I don't know where he is, he wouldn't care anyway—I'm the only one cared about my little girl, and you cops can't say I didn't, whatever—"

"Mrs. Thomas," said Maddox, "this is going to end up as a charge of Murder Two at least, so suppose we take some shortcuts and forget all the theatricals. Rex seems to have slightly more sense—he didn't show up at the job tonight. Have you been in touch with him?" She shook her head just once. "Was it Rex who used the lighted cigarettes on Peggy?"

"Nobody'd do anything like that—what do you mean, *murder?* Nobody murdered—"

"Come on, come on. Was it Rex?"

She snuffled into the handkerchief, and after a minute, not looking up, she said sullenly, "I don't s'pose you got any kids. You got to teach them how to act, punish them sometimes. I—well, sure, Rex gave her a little spanking, time or two, she got out of hand. That's all. At least, I never saw him do anything bad to her—just, you know, spanked her." She looked at him defiantly.

"I see. And you said she fell downstairs? Where? Did you see it happen?"

"Well, uh, no, I wasn't there. It was last night, I guess. At Gail's place. Rex took her there, we were going out—"

"And this morning you realized she was hurt enough to need a doctor."

"Yeah, that's right. Nobody meant to hurt her, anyway if Rex ever did I never knew about it and you can't prove I did.

How do I know—cops say anything—I never saw Rex do nothing to her, naturally I wouldn't have let him if I did—"

And that was the expectable line for her to take.

In the kitchen, D'Arcy leaned on the refrigerator and regarded his four captives thoughtfully. The girls were both blond and thin, one smartly dressed in a brown suit, high heels, the other one in a pink pantsuit. The two men were in fairly good sports clothes, and if both had lobe-length hair it was neatly combed; both were clean-shaven. As people went these days, they were a respectable-looking quartet; he would guess, in decent jobs, not idle bums. Of course, friends of Candy's; but on the surface, Candy was a fairly ordinary type, too, holding a job. They eyed him back silently, and he asked conversationally, "You've heard about Mrs. Thomas' little girl?"

Gail Andrews said, "Yeah—an awful thing. A real tragedy. She was a cute kid."

"Just falling downstairs, Candy said," put in Doris Hobson. "I suppose she hit her head or something."

They would have been here awhile, and it wasn't in the cards that Candy hadn't told them about the cops. "Any of you see her fall down? Where was it supposed to have happened?"

Silence, and then Gail said, "Well, at my place, I said they could leave her there while they went out. Rex said she fell down the stairs."

"You didn't notice there was anything wrong with her then? How long was she there?"

"I don't know—until about eleven, I guess. She wasn't any bother, she went to sleep."

"You know," said D'Arcy abruptly, "it's going to get filed as Murder Two. So it'd be interesting to know if any of you know anything that ought to come out. You're all pretty good friends of Candy's—of Rex Slaney? You get together here pretty often?"

They shared glances. The Hobson girl said in a subdued voice, "I guess you could say. On account of the kid, kind of a drag, Candy couldn't always leave her, and besides our place's even smaller than this—and Rex—"

"So you had the chance to see how Rex behaved to the kid. Did any of you ever see him hit her? Slap her around?"

They were silent. "Murder Two," said D'Arcy, though he wasn't at all sure it wouldn't end up as manslaughter. "I don't suppose any of you would like to get roped in as accessories."

"Listen, for God's sake," said Jim Hobson hoarsely, "what the hell business of ours—yeah, I'd seen him knock the kid around some, what the hell, kids ask for it, my old man did it to me—"

"Like, they need to be burned with live cigarettes?"

"I saw him do that once," said Gail in a shaky small voice. "I guess Rex kind of resented Peggy, you know. I guess the only reason he never moved in with Candy was the kid—there wasn't room, only one bedroom. Well, no, I didn't like seeing him do that, but I—"

"It didn't occur to you to do anything about it?"

"Listen, it wasn't my kid—and Candy was right there, it was up to her to tell him to stop it. I just walked out."

"Anybody else?" asked D'Arcy.

After another long minute King said, "Well, one night he took his belt to her—but kids—she'd got chocolate all over his best pants, and he— Well, like Gail says, it wasn't our kid, and what the hell?"

D'Arcy regarded them impassively, average specimens of urban humanity, and said, "We'll want you to come in and make statements." They snarled at him. "And you may be asked to testify at any trial."

King came out with obscenities. "Wasting time—lose a week's pay, sit around some lousy court! Damn cops—"

Which was conceivably why they'd shut their eyes in the first place. D'Arcy left the cramped, slovenly kitchen with its sinkful of dirty dishes and in the living room found that Maddox had reduced Candy to floods of tears.

"I think we've got enough," said Maddox.

"In spades," said D'Arcy. As he switched on the ignition of the Dodge he added, "I'm sometimes tempted to think all those earnest fundamentalists are right—the Lord about to fetch down destruction. Not without reason."

At the station they found Ken Donaldson yawning over a paperback; he said Dick was out on an attempted assault. He heard about Peggy with a grimace. "Thanks, I'll take night watch—the nice straightforward hit-runs and bar brawls and heists mostly all we get."

Maddox put out an A.P.B. on Slaney, after the computer at Sacramento told them he was driving a four-year-old Datsun, plate number thus and such; and then they went home.

At the little house behind the Clintons' larger house on Gregory Avenue, he found Sue sitting up in bed wielding a hair dryer. Unprecedently he went out to build himself a drink before telling her about Candy.

On Saturday morning Rodriguez was back and Feinman off. Dabney and Rowan still had work to do at the Peller house, and Maddox and Rodriguez trailed along to finish looking around there. It was still raining but in a half-hearted way, as if it were thinking of quitting.

"Did you say money?" said Rodriguez, looking around the living room with its thin rug and old furniture.

"The neighbors said. I kind of doubt it."

"One thing"—Rodriguez smoothed his neat mustache—"it doesn't look as if there was any cunning involved. He broke in and killed her, pawed through everything, and *vamos*. Is there any way of knowing what he might have got?"

"We don't know yet. And one slug fired from the gun. I wonder if she winged him?"

"It's seldom that easy," said Rodriguez.

"Sometimes fate's on our side, César."

Rowan came in from the bedroom balancing an address book in one hand. "Maybe give you some people to talk to. I've dusted it. But he's left us quite a lot to go on, Ivor. One nice thing about rain—his shoes were muddy, and he left some dandy footprints on the kitchen floor. About size ten, a distinctive sole pattern—we'll get casts—and either coming or going he left a piece of shirt, I think it is, caught on the screen door. Green plaid flannel. See what the lab says about it. And I've got a sample of all the blood—if any of it's a different type than hers, it could say she did wing him."

Maddox was leafing through the notebook. There weren't

many names in it, and all female except one, Alexander Barton, an address on Hollywood Boulevard—a business address, then. "So you can go talk to some of these," and he handed the book to Rodriguez. "I'll look up Barton." They left Rowan and Dabney still pottering around with brushes and magnifying glasses.

The Hollywood address was on the top floor of a bank building, and the office door bore the legend A. M. BARTON, ATTORNEY AT LAW. It was locked. Naturally, on a Saturday. Maddox found a public phone, looked in the book, and found a home address up in Laurel Canyon. Barton was home, intrigued at a call from police, and proffered any assistance he could give. Maddox drove up there through lessening rain and was welcomed into a rather elegantly furnished living room in a big two-story Spanish house. "Offer you a cup of coffee—did you say, Sergeant? What can I do for you?"

Maddox accepted the coffee gratefully and told him about Mrs. Peller. "We found your name in her address book."

"Murdered?" said Barton, horrified. He was a plump, prosperous-looking elderly man. "Well, for God's sake. The last person—but I suppose that's always the reaction. Margaret Peller—and so she never did make that will after all— I hadn't seen or heard of her for years till just last week—"

"We heard something about money. Had she any, Mr. Barton?"

"Poor as the proverbial church mouse," said Barton promptly. "It all went. I handled the thing for her husband, Charles Peller. He was badly injured on the job at Lockheed, this was twelve, thirteen years back, and permanently disabled. No, there wasn't any suit—it was an obvious accident, the company liable, and they paid up with no question. It was a sizable settlement—a hundred thousand, but it had all gone taking care of him. I hadn't laid eyes on the woman since, until she came to see me last week about making a will. She told me then it was all gone. He was permanently paralyzed, had to be in a convalescent home, and therapy, the various specialists over that period—he died last year, and it was mostly gone then. I've got some notes at the office— she said there was about five thousand in a savings account, and aside from that she had her Social Security, a few savings from the days he was still working. Oh, and they owned the house."

"You were drawing up a will?"

"Not yet, actually. She said she'd come in this week, there wasn't all that great hurry—" Barton shook his head. "We never do know. She wasn't really old—sixty-five. They'd never had any children, but she had a niece, living in Pittsburgh, she wanted everything to go to her."

"Mmh," said Maddox. "As far as you know, she hadn't been threatened by anyone? Didn't express any fear of anyone she knew—in the neighborhood?"

Barton stared at him. "Of course not. Excuse me, Sergeant, that seems a strange question—of course I'm not a criminal lawyer, but—from what you tell me, some lout just broke in and attacked her, ransacked the house. It's not likely it was anybody she knew."

"Well, we have to go by experience," said Maddox absently, "and it is a fact, Mr. Barton, that in about eight out of ten homicides the guilty party is known to the victim—relative, friend, next-door neighbor. At least this tells us a little more."

He went back to the station to see if Rodriguez was back. He wasn't. Maddox left a note for him to meet him at the Grotto and went out for lunch.

Sue had found Pauline Strange's boy friend at home this morning, and the whole setup on that was looking funnier. Bill Blackwell seemed to be a good type, eldest in a large and evidently happy family. This was a big rambling old house perched on top of a hill overlooking Hollywood, and Mrs. Blackwell had welcomed her hospitably, a still-pretty frosted blonde. "It's about Pauline, if you're police—goodness, how interesting they sent a policewoman—we've all been wondering about it, since Mr. Strange called Thursday night—not that Bill could have told them anything if we'd known where he was then, as a matter of fact he was at the Ledbetters'—it's really very queer, I can't imagine what can have happened, a very sweet girl really—" Her eyes were curious on Sue. "You'll want to see Bill. Just don't mind all the noise, with eight chil-

dren cooped up it's bound to be noisy— I'll shoo them out of
the living room, you can talk there—"

And now, in the big living room with its comfortably
shabby furniture, a few toys scattered around, a large
dignified elderly Saint Bernard asleep in front of the fire, and
subdued noises from the rest of the house, Bill Blackwell was
impressing her as honest and straightforward.

"I'm as much in the dark as the Stranges, Mrs. Maddox," he
said. "I couldn't tell you a thing. The last time I saw Pauline
was Wednesday night, we were out on a double date together." Bill was a big fellow, looking older than his nineteen
years; he had a surprisingly short crop of dark hair, very blue
eyes like his mother's, wide shoulders. "We went to a movie
and then had a snack at a Shakeys'—just an ordinary sort of
date. It was about a quarter past twelve when we dropped
Pauline off at home, she was a little worried because she
wasn't supposed to be later than midnight. She was just"—he
gestured helplessly—"her usual self. Just talking about usual
things."

"I see," said Sue. There wasn't anything to get hold of on
this at all. Unlike most of what they saw during the daily routine, it was just a mystery. Pauline might have been snatched
up by a flying saucer. "Who were you with?" she asked at random.

"Oh, Jim Warden and his girl. It was the first time we'd
double-dated with them, I haven't known Jim long, he's in one
of my classes. The girl's name's Patty Lowell, she seems like a
nice kid."

"Mrs. Strange said there was some talk about you and
Pauline getting engaged."

He flushed. "No, we're not. She wanted to be—" The flush
grew deeper, and he said, "Hell, that sounds—all wrong. I
don't want you to think—but Pauline—well, she's a sweet kid
and I love her, but sometimes she doesn't use common sense. I
mean, I want us to get married, too, sometime. She knows
that. But I'm just in my first year at college, I'm studying law,
and even when I get through and pass the Bar, it might be a
while before I'm earning very much. Enough to support a
wife and—and a family. Pauline wants us to get married as
soon as she graduates from high, but I can't see it. She says

she could get a job, help out, but it's not sense, you can see that. Rent's so high now, and everything else. And—and I don't think it's all the way fair to her, get engaged. She's not eighteen, she might meet somebody else. I guess"—and he smiled—"you can say we're sort of half engaged."

Sue cocked her head at him. "You don't know what happened to her—but you're not worried much?"

He was silent, head bent over his clasped hands. "I think she's O.K.," he said.

"The Stranges don't."

"Look," he said. He got up and wandered over to the window, stood with his back to her. "I know. They were in a tizzy, Mother said, trying to get me Thursday night. They thought maybe she'd called me, we were out somewhere together. At that time of night. I wasn't even home—I had an exam coming up, I'd gone over to Bob Ledbetter's to study. It gets kind of noisy around here sometimes. I—no, I don't know anything, but I'm not worried because—the way Sylvia told me it happened, Pauline had to take off somewhere of her own accord, didn't she? There wasn't any sign that—that she'd been attacked or kidnaped or anything."

"No. So where do you think she is?" asked Sue.

"Oh, hell," he said unhappily. "This sounds—I don't *know*. But Pauline can be as—as stubborn as hell. And she's been going on about this marriage bit, and—well, we've had some arguments. And I don't want to sound like the world's biggest egotist, but I've got an idea she's just taken off somewhere to scare me. Scare us. Because the Stranges are on my side, they want us to wait too. And it's only, what, a little over a day."

"Where do you think she could have gone? The family says she wouldn't have had much money—ten or twenty dollars."

"I wouldn't know that. But she could be with some girl she knows at school—"

"We've talked to her closest friend. And besides, all of those girls would be living at home with their parents—"

"No, no, I mean this one girl. Brenda Hansen. She was new in school this term, Pauline talked about her a lot. She was—interested because this Brenda was—well, different. I didn't much like the sound of her, but Pauline—"

"Different how?"

"Oh, she hasn't got a regular family, her parents are dead, she lives with an uncle, and the way Pauline told it, he doesn't care what time she comes home or what she does or anything. Pauline kind of admired this chick, and—well, you know girls"—he grinned at her—"about sticking together. If Pauline wanted to—make us all think something had happened to her, well, you see what I mean—"

"But you haven't tried to contact this girl?"

"I only thought about it this morning," he said rather miserably. "How could I? I don't know where she lives."

Sue regarded him thoughtfully. It could be one explanation. And as she'd expected, more background had filled in a little. The more she heard about Pauline Strange, the more she was inclined to think Pauline was a scatterbrain.

Rodriguez didn't show up at the Grotto, but drifted in about the middle of the afternoon with a handful of nothing. All the other names in the address book had turned out to be friends of Margaret Peller's, mostly old friends; none of them had seen her in the past week, but they had told him this and that.

"The niece is Mrs. Norman Atwill—the one out-of-state address in the book. They all said she didn't have much jewelry —a little costume stuff, a garnet pin and bracelet that belonged to her grandmother, her wedding ring, engagement ring—vague descriptions, not good enough for the pawnbrokers' list. The only other thing they said is that she was a spunky old girl. Not nervous about living alone—she always said, anybody tried to break in on her, she had her husband's gun and wasn't afraid to use it." Rodriguez sat down at his desk and lit a cigarette. "Which she apparently did."

"Yes," said Maddox. He picked up the phone and asked Whitwell to get him somebody on the Pittsburgh force. Eventually he was connected with a Lieutenant Eisensohn, explained, asked them to notify the niece. "And," he added, putting down the phone, "that bar is now open where Juanita picked up Rutherford on Thursday night. Inefficient cops—we never got to it yesterday, and it's probably a question of going through the motions, but we ought to go and ask. Just in case anybody there knows her."

"I am not," said Rodriguez lazily, "so very damn concerned about catching up to Juanita. The johns were asking for it— they always are. But I suppose we'd better." He took a paperback out of his raincoat pocket and laid it on the desk; it was a fat tome of a historical novel with a dramatic cover.

"You're off the detective novels?" asked Maddox. Some time ago, Rodriguez had been introduced to some of the classics in the field; and as D'Arcy had grumbled, while he was working his way through John Dickson Carr especially, he might as well have stayed home for all the use he'd been.

"I tell you, Ivor," said Rodriguez seriously, "the people writing them now—the new ones—well, they just can't measure up. After I'd read all the old ones, I tried some of that, and I might as well be reading my own case reports. They aren't interested in mysteries these days, only what they call realism. No more glamour or suspense than in the real job."

Maddox threw his head back and laughed. "How right you are. Fashions in these things, I suppose, and the ignorant civilians find it interesting to read all about police procedure, but I'll never know why. Just occasionally we get something a little offbeat, but very seldom mysterious, and in lo, these many years I can't recall anything remotely glamorous, if that's a word for it. Come on, we'd better go talk to that bartender."

The bartender, of course, had not noticed Juanita or Rutherford, and her description didn't ring any bells. The waitress who had served them remembered Juanita because of her clothes, but said she wouldn't recognize a picture. Rutherford had agreed to look at some mug shots tomorrow. The other johns had all looked, too, and hadn't picked any out, but they had to go by the book; and you never knew, some people were sharper-eyed than others.

At the outset, of course, they had looked in records for Juanita and her M.O., and come up with a blank. There were a few pedigrees of the whores who, perhaps parsimonious, had lured johns up to the male confederates' guns or fists. It was conceivable that such a one had decided to go it alone instead of sharing the loot; but none of those in records conformed to the description. The routine could take them just so far.

They were not aware, of course, that in the midst of the sordid and unmysterious crimes normal to their city beat, they were about to be handed a real gem of an offbeat one.

It stopped raining at six-fifteen as Maddox was driving home, but the heavens were still dark. When he caught the light at Vine and Santa Monica, there were black headlines on the corner newsstand: "NEW STORM TO COME."

Sue had beaten him home, and was changing into a housedress. "I'm going to cream the rest of that turkey roast. Over toast or baked potatoes?"

"Potatoes."

"Then we won't eat for an hour. Mother goes on raving over that microwave oven of Aunt Evelyn's—you can bake potatoes in about seven minutes—but they're too expensive."

"Give us time for a leisurely civilized drink. Where were you all afternoon?"

"Chasing a wild goose. And yet I don't know—it's possible, I suppose." She filled him in on Pauline as she put in the potatoes and diced turkey in cream sauce. "I routed out the school registrar—she was annoyed—to get this Hansen girl's address. Granting that she's the kind to go along, it's exactly the kind of silly stunt Pauline might pull—make everybody think something dire had happened to her, so when she turns up safe and sound they'd fall over themselves to do whatever she wanted. She's a flibbertigibbet," said Sue. "Oh, a nice girl— nice family—but a little scatterbrained like her mother. The other girl took after her father—common sense."

"And what does the Hansen girl say?" asked Maddox, measuring gin.

"I didn't find her. The uncle she lives with—at a mansion up on Franklin—has his own plane and they've gone to Acapulco for the weekend, left on Friday morning. I do wonder if Pauline's with them. What I heard from the one neighbor I saw, he sounds the kind of man who'd say, 'Sure, bring anybody you want, doll.' He's something in TV." She accepted the martini and sipped. "Well, I suppose time will tell."

Most of Sunday, with Daisy and Rowan off and Sergeant Buck sitting on the desk, they had the witnesses coming in, willing and unwilling, to make the formal statements. There had been another liquor store heist last night, a freeway crash with two dead, but for Saturday night in Hollywood it had been mercifully quiet.

Feinman, D'Arcy, and Sue spent some time with Candy Thomas and her friends, getting chapter and verse down in black and white. Candy was very much aware now that she might share some charge, and answers had to be pulled out of her with infinite patience. The A.P.B. hadn't turned up Rex Slaney yet. Sometime today or tomorrow they should get the autopsy report on Peggy.

Maddox took two witnesses downtown to headquarters, Rutherford and the owner of the liquor store heisted on Thursday night, Wilbur Tallman. In the R. and I. office a pretty flaxen-haired policewoman fetched in some relevant fat books of mug shots, and they settled down to look at them.

Half an hour later Rutherford said suddenly, "Now that looks like her," and Maddox snapped to attention, coming to look. The mug shot showed a strikingly handsome light-skinned Negro girl with a smooth high pompadour and sultry eyes. He scanned the pedigree. Terri Lee Wilson, twenty-eight, five-five, a hundred and twenty, black and brown. Soliciting, bad checks, D. and D.— "It *isn't* her," said Rutherford, "but this one's the same type, Sergeant, see? A real classy looker, nothing cheap, real smooth. Not like the usual crumby chick on the make. This type. Could be Mex, part Oriental maybe." He went on leafing over pages.

Forty minutes after that Tallman said gleefully, "That's him! I knew if he was here I'd spot him, and that's him!" Maddox looked. Donald William Casey, male Caucasian, six feet, a hundred and sixty, brown and blue, no marks. The pedigree was expectable: shoplifting, B. and E., armed robbery, assault with intent. He was five months out of Folsom and supposedly still on parole.

"O.K., thanks very much," said Maddox, and found a phone

to call the office. An A.P.B. went out on Casey; Sacramento said no car was registered to him. He went up to Welfare and Rehab to find out who Casey's parole officer was, and discovered that Casey had officially gone off parole last week, which figured just fine. The stupid little lout's not always so stupid. If they pulled something while they were still on P.A., no red tape about shoving them back in the joint; if they were off P.A., there'd be every chance of plea bargaining, a lesser charge, the chance to make bail.

Rutherford didn't find Juanita in the books. "Jeez, I'd like to see you pick her up, that little cheating bitch. I was so goddamned surprised—real classy-looking chick like that, pull a gun on me—"

"Well, we appreciate your trying, Mr. Rutherford."

Maddox had had a sandwich at the canteen at headquarters. He got back to Wilcox Street at two o'clock. Another burglary had been reported, and Ellis was talking to the bereaved citizen. Sue, Feinman, and D'Arcy were still busy with the statements.

Rodriguez was sitting at his desk looking thoughtful. "I'll try it on you," he said as Maddox came up. "Would it be any use to look up men Charles Peller knew at Lockheed? Who knew he'd got that settlement? Might have thought he had some left? That the widow—"

Maddox shook his head. "Your torturous mind, César. Really reaching. Thirteen years back, and besides"—he sat down, passed a hand over his jaw, which could have stood another shave by this hour—"only an idiot would have expected her to keep much cash in the house, even if she had any. Wait for the lab reports."

"Unless she was known to distrust banks—more and more people do. Only, of course, what you got from the lawyer—" Rodriguez shrugged.

The outside phone rang and Maddox picked it up. "Wilcox Street Police Station, Sergeant Maddox."

"Gonzales. I don't know what you can do about this—this mess, but I guess you ought to look at it. Jesus and Mary, Sergeant, you never saw such a mess. And this poor old guy— Sergeant, I damn near cried to hear him—if we can do anything—"

Patrolman Ramon Gonzales was a hard-bitten professional cop, on the force fourteen years, and not easily moved to maudlin sympathy for crime victims. Maddox was surprised. "What's the complaint? Address?"

"It's La Mirada Avenue. Just behind the junior high school, and if I had to guess—oh, Jesus and Mary, you never saw such a thing—you'd better come have a look, Sergeant."

CHAPTER 3

La Mirada Avenue was in the heart of Hollywood. A couple of blocks up on Fountain, that secondary main drag, the old houses had been torn down and the jerry-built, garishly painted new apartments had gone up; farther west and north, business had taken over some former residential areas. But in these quiet narrow old side streets the little houses had remained, neighborhoods largely unchanged: modest old stucco and frame houses on standard fifty by one hundred and fifty-foot lots, inviolate if aged; some were neatly maintained, a few neglected.

The one they wanted was marked by the black and white squad car in the drive. It was the neatest, trimmest house on this block, a frame bungalow spanking white with green trim around the windows, and the landscaping looked almost professional, two patches of deep green lawn, a trimmed privet hedge lining the curving walk to the porch, well-kept rose beds on each side of that.

There were a few neighbors out, a knot of people on the sidewalk across the street, more on the lawn next door, Patrolman Gonzales standing above the squad car with two men and a woman. Maddox pulled the Maserati up behind the squad, and Gonzales came to meet them. The woman and one of the men up there were young, the other, a smallish old man, just standing, unmoving.

"What've we got?" asked Maddox.

"I couldn't describe it," said Gonzales. "That's the owner, the old fellow there—Anton Czerny. All I've got—after I saw it—I got from the other ones, young couple live two doors down, Doug Wyler and his wife. Czerny—he's a widower. He and his wife got out of Czechoslovakia just after the war, probably by the skin of their teeth. Had one daughter. The old man's worked for Parks and Recreation for thirty years, landscape gardener, retired a couple of years ago. Then his wife died. My God, Sergeant, it makes you wonder, the things that happen to people—what did the old man ever do to deserve it?" Gonzales took off his cap and wiped his forehead.

"Such as?"

"You can see how he's kept up the house—" Gonzales nodded at the lawns, the neatly trimmed hedge, and blooming roses. "The daughter wasn't married, librarian lived in Chicago, and a while ago she came down with leukemia. Three, four months to live. He went back there to be with her, last February. Made an arrangement with a friend in Parks and Rec to come and cut the grass, water, keep up the yard. He closed up the house and went. The daughter died about a week ago, and after he'd arranged the funeral and settled things up, he came home. Just today. Got here an hour ago and— You go and look," said Gonzales.

The front door of the house stood open. Maddox and Rodriguez started up past the squad car. The young man, Doug Wyler, had one arm around the old man's shoulders. He was a broad, sandy young fellow, nondescript face drawn with anger and sympathy. Young Mrs. Wyler seemed to be crying. The old man was looking straight ahead, his eyes dazed.

Maddox pushed the front door wider with automatic care for possible prints. After thirty seconds he said, "Good God almighty!"

"*¡Jesús, María y José!*" echoed Rodriguez.

The living room, directly beyond the door, was a chaos of mindless destruction; it was impossible to imagine what it had been. The carpet shredded in strips, one overstuffed chair with all its stuffing pulled out, upholstery cut to pieces, legs hacked off; other furniture hacked apart, a small TV smashed utterly flat, shards of glass ground into the floor, the sofa with all its padding gouged out, and everywhere—floor, furniture, mantel—a mess of stale, spoiling food, remnants of hamburgers, pizzas, french fries, mustard, catchup—cans of soft drinks spilled here and there. Above that was another stench; in one corner of the room was a pile of human excrement.

There were ants by the million all over the spoiling food. "My
God," said Maddox, and moved cautiously beyond the living
room.

The whole little house had been systematically, viciously,
and thoroughly vandalized. There wasn't a whole piece of furniture left except the refrigerator, overturned on the kitchen
floor with the freezer door off. In every room there were great
gouges dug out of the ceiling, exposing the laths. All the
wallpaper in the hall and both bedrooms had been peeled off
in random strips, the walls slashed deeply, and plaster dug out
in great holes. The toilet in the main bath had been wrenched
bodily from its connections, overturned, and hammered into
three pieces; the wash basin there had been smashed away
from its pipes and lay on top of the toilet. In the kitchen the
linoleum had been slashed into ruin, the floorboards beneath
splintered. A half bath in the service porch had been as
ruthlessly attacked, toilet and basin broken apart. The two
small bedrooms were heaped with more destruction, hacked-
apart furniture, slashed mattresses, torn-up clothes. In there,
and in the kitchen, were more dirty plates of uneaten rotten
food, more ants, and in one bedroom another pile of excrement. Smells vied with each other.

"*¡Vaya por Dios!*" said Rodriguez numbly. "What was loose
here?"

"Emissaries of Satan, it looks like," said Maddox, "and I
don't think we've got their prints on file, César." He threaded
his way back to the living room and looked around. Beside a
paper plate on the mantel was a crumpled paper bag: others
were scattered here and there. He investigated three, dis-
carded them, held on to the fourth after sniffing it deeply. He
handed it to Rodriguez. "Maybe some more around."

"The grass," said Rodriguez. "Which figures."

"There's a junior high school across the street."

"*¡Santa María!*" said Rodriguez. "Twelve- to fifteen-year-
olds?"

"You've been a cop too long to be surprised." Maddox went
out and took a breath of fresh air gratefully, walked down to
where the little group stood in the drive. For the first time he
noticed that the old man was holding in his hands a small
steel box, the kind of box supposed to protect important

papers from fire. Czerny was not a big man, thin and a little
stooped, nearly bald. He was probably wearing his best suit,
an old-fashioned gray herringbone with a vest. He was still
staring straight ahead with dazed eyes.

"Please, come into our place, Mr. Czerny," young Mrs.
Wyler was pleading. "Sit down—a cup of coffee—"

"You can stay with us till it's fixed up." Wyler looked at
Maddox. "Jesus Christ, did you ever see—we never heard a
damn thing, but the house next door's been empty six months
—I can't get over—I just hope to God you get whoever did
it—"

Maddox said noncommittally, "We can try," and headed
around to the back. Gonzales went with him.

"I had a look. I said I could have a guess— Kids! Kids from
the school. And they were smart enough not to do any damage to the outside of the place, so nobody suspected what was
going on. Everything looked perfectly O.K. to the guy who
came to cut the lawn and so on. You can see—"

Maddox could. There was a single detached garage, with a
side door. Through the small window he could see an old
Ford pick-up truck, set up on blocks. "Wonder why they
didn't fool with that," said Gonzales, "but I suppose the tank's
empty, maybe they found that out."

There was a nearly new screen door at the back of the
house, hiding the solid wooden door. When Maddox tried the
screen door he could see that its hook had been pulled out,
the wooden door forcibly broken in; it swung open at a touch.
There was a fairly good Yale lock, but no dead bolt.

"And don't I know, not one goddamn thing we can do about
it," said Gonzales savagely. "The juveniles—we can't print 'em
even when they've done something— My God, it'd be easier to
burn the place down and rebuild, that *mess*—and that poor
old man, all alone in the world—all he had left, probably—"

Maddox said heavily, "It's a bastard all right." He walked
back around the side of the house, where another bed of roses
bloomed, and approached the now silent little group. "Mr.
Czerny—"

The old man looked up slowly. His eyes were unfocused,
and then at Wyler's renewed touch he blinked and held up his

little box. "Mr. Czerny, these are policemen," said Wyler. "They want to help—" But he sounded a little helpless.

"Police?" repeated Czerny. "But that is worst part." He looked at his box. "So long we studied, it was hard, the English—but, to be Americans—and the better life for our little Anna—and at last we get the papers. The papers for citizenship. And now—now the papers are gone, all torn up—somewhere there"—he nodded at the house—"and I cannot be a citizen anymore, they will send me back to the Communists."

The Wylers burst into impetuous reassurance and explanation, but he only looked at his empty box. "And all the pictures—all the family pictures we had, from long ago, parents, brothers, sisters, all the pictures of our little Anna since she was baby—all gone, all torn up—nothing to remember by at all left now."

"Mr. Czerny," said Maddox gently.

Slowly his eyes fixed on Maddox' face. "Police?" he said. "But could you tell me perhaps—why? Why does any do such things to my house? To an old man never does harm to any? Police—I will tell you, even back there—then—when the Communists come to search houses, take away people to prison, they do not make such destructions. It is only wild animals make such destructions, I tell you." He dropped the box and raised both hands to his face.

Gonzales' shift ended at four o'clock, and he wouldn't mind quitting today. In fourteen years on this force he'd seen a lot of grief and trouble and blood, but that was one of the worst things he'd seen. He wouldn't forget it in a hurry, and the hell of it was, there probably wasn't much the front-office brains could do about it. It would be good to get home, and out of uniform, and see Elisa and the kids, and relax a little.

He turned the squad onto Santa Monica, heading for Wilcox Street, and just as he got to the corner of Cahuenga a young woman ran out to the curb and waved at him violently. He pulled over into the red zone and she came running around to the driver's side.

"Somebody stole something from my car, Officer!" She was a pretty redhead, excited and upset. "In the market lot—it couldn't be three minutes ago, I only went in to get cigarettes—"

Gonzales got out and she led him up into the lot, half running. "It's the Honda right there—I didn't bother to lock it, only be gone a couple of minutes—and oh, my goodness, I just thought—I bet I know why—"

"What was stolen, miss?" asked Gonzales. He was resigned; the necessary report would delay his getting home by half an hour.

She started to laugh then, giggling and leaning on the car. "This is going to sound pretty silly, but I can't help it—it was a box of d-dirt—"

"A box of *dirt?*" said Gonzales.

"Yes, and I j-just remembered, he put it in a carton l-labeled D-Dewar's Scotch and it's all neatly taped—oh, dear!" she gasped. "You must think I'm absolutely nuts, I'm sorry. But the elevator's on the fritz—at the building where I work—and they've got it up to the roof to work on it and just saw horses at the landings—and yesterday afternoon I lost the diamond from my engagement ring, I'd just come out of the office with Ella and I've got this habit of gesturing and the darn thing just went swoosh down the elevator shaft, I saw it go—I knew it was loose, I'd meant to get it fixed. And the superintendent was so nice, he shoveled up all the gunk at the bottom of the shaft so I could look for it, he called this morning so I went down to get it—"

Gonzales began to laugh too. "Well, look, miss, maybe whoever took it didn't keep it long if he found out. Let's have a look around."

"It weighed a ton, but if he thought it was a case of scotch he'd expect it to, wouldn't he?" They started to look around the lot. There was a fair-sized crowd coming and going; people looked at them with faint curiosity. Ten minutes later Gonzales spotted the box pushed half under some bushes at the far end of the lot. "That the one?"

"Thank goodness, that's it!"

The tape had been partly torn away from the lid of the carton. Gonzales said, "I'll bet he stopped to have a quick look when it didn't rattle."

"Whatever, at least I've got it. You're an angel," she said fervently. "Of all the crazy things!"

Gonzales carried it back to the Honda. "I just hope you find the diamond, miss."

"So do I—and thanks a million!"

Gonzales went on to the station, feeling slightly better.

Maddox went back to the office about four o'clock, leaving Rodriguez poking around taking notes and talking to shocked neighbors. When the neighbors hadn't heard anything, they probably wouldn't be much help; or would they? They'd know the neighborhood kids; but it needn't have been neighborhood kids.

And Rodriguez said bitterly, just what good would it do the old man if they did drop on the kids who had done it? A charge of vandalism, even such monumental destruction—not a felony, and carrying a possible sentence of a fine and probation—nothing more for juveniles.

He came into the office, glancing across the landing where Sue was on the phone looking preoccupied. George Ellis was hunched over his typewriter, cussing as he changed the ribbon.

"This is a hell of a town, you know," said Maddox without sitting down. "A dirty greedy town with a hell of a lot of dirty greedy no-good louts and bums in it. High and low, from the beautiful people sniffing coke and swapping bed partners every night to the riffraff heisting honest storekeepers and rolling the drunks, at the bottom."

"Hah?" said Ellis. "Oh, goddamn the damn machine!" He dropped the ribbon and it rolled merrily away to the corner of the room.

"But we've got to have faith," said Maddox, staring out the window to where the sky was now serenely blue, "or what's the point of doing the damn job at all? Faith, that in any town, any time, there are more nice people than the bastards." He laughed suddenly, sat down at his desk, and picked up the phone.

He happened to know that just about now, in the studio of the local TV channel, the rushes of tonight's news hour were being reviewed. The L.A.P.D. was always as polite as possible to TV news people; they never knew when they might find it useful. Maddox was patient and perseverant. Yes, he realized that Mr. Dale's time was valuable, he only wanted five minutes of it. Mr. Dale (he crossed his fingers) had always been co-operative with the police. He thought Mr. Dale would be interested in a little human-interest story. Yes, he would hold on.

Presently the great man condescended to talk to him.

He was slightly cheered up when Sue's mother dropped in and stayed to dinner. He and Mrs. Carstairs got on fine. They talked about Peggy and Pauline when they got onto shop talk at all, and he didn't mention Anton Czerny.

They both looked up in surprise when he went over and turned on the seldom-used portable TV at two minutes of ten. "What on earth?" said Sue. "If you're wondering about the weather, they're never right anyway. Talking about a new storm."

"I'm just curious," said Maddox, "to see if that bleeding-heart liberal recognizes a real human-interest story." He listened to ten minutes of international news without comment. After a commercial the great man flashed back onto the screen looking suitably wise, and a banner above his beautifully silvered coiffure announced "The Local Scene."

"Closer to home, your news staff only this afternoon stumbled upon a small tragedy which perhaps symbolizes the tragedy of the modern city—our city and all cities—in the crime-ridden times we all live in today. We bring you some exclusive scenes filmed today in the heart of Hollywood." A nice shot of the trim little house with its green lawn and roses flashed on. "At noon today Mr. Anton Czerny, seventy-two, an immigrant to America after the Second World War, returned home. He returned from the tragedy of losing his only child to a dread disease, and alone in the world returned to tragedy—"

"He can throw it," said Maddox, and reached to switch it off, but Mrs. Carstairs stopped him.

"Good heavens, that house—" The photographs were mercilessly revealing, in full color. "My lord, Sue, look at it—"

"Was that what you went out on?" asked Sue, looking in horror.

"For my sins. Old windbag," said Maddox as the great man droned on. "But quite a few people do take him seriously. Something might come of it."

On Monday morning they were doubly shorthanded: Dabney was off and Daisy in court at that narco trial. Sue went directly up to Hollywood High, hoping to chase down Brenda Hansen.

Maddox had just got in and was looking over the night-watch report; neither Casey nor Slaney had been turned up by the A.P.B.'s, and it seemed to have been a quiet night. He was interrupted by a messenger who brought in a couple of autopsy reports from Dr. Bergner's office. Peggy, and who the hell was Albert A. Trissle?

He looked at the one on Peggy first, shoving it across to Rodriguez page by page. It made depressing reading. Details of the external injuries: burns, bruises, estimates of when sustained. Ruptured spleen, damaged liver, skull fracture. Cause of death, massive concussion complicated by internal bleeding. It wasn't any surprise, but not nice.

"And wouldn't it be gratifying if the judge threw the book at him," said Rodriguez. "But I won't hold my breath. And who sicked our local opinion-maker onto Czerny?"

"Three guesses," said Maddox.

"You still have some faith in human nature?"

"Some. I—for God's sake!" said Maddox. He was reading the other autopsy report. He hadn't heard the man's name—this was the D.O.A. found on Thursday night. Albert Trissle, aged fifty-four. And so far from passing out decently from a heart attack, he'd been stabbed to death. "Joe," said Maddox, "you were on this one—here's a little surprise for us. And some more legwork."

"What?" Feinman ambled over and took the report. "Stabbed? For God's sake—I never saw the body, but by Dick's report there wasn't a mark on him, looked like a natural death. That's a funny one."

"A long thin blade," Maddox pointed out, translating from

Bergner's more technical phraseology, "no external bleeding. I will be damned."

"And why in hell he had to be half a block away from where he should've been," said Feinman, annoyed, "is just our bad luck. He was barely inside L.A.P.D. territory—you know the United Artists Studio marks the boundary, that piece of county along the Strip."

"What's that got to do with it?"

"He was night security guard there. One of four. The others missed him about eleven o'clock and called the sheriff, but it was one of our cars spotted him half a block down Sunset. It looked plain as day. He was on his break, and ran out of cigarettes or something and started down to the all-night drugstore at the corner, and had a fit."

"Only now it seems he didn't," said Maddox. "Was he robbed?"

"I never saw him, I tell you. I told the morgue to return the personal effects to the wife. It didn't look like anything," said Feinman. "Hell, I'd better call her. His car was in the studio lot, she said she'd come get that."

Over the phone, Mrs. Trissle was plaintive. "Well, they haven't sent me anything, Mr. Feinman, no. But I know there's a lot of red tape when these things happen, I didn't want to bother you. Bert wouldn't have had much money on him, but of course I'll need his papers—Social Security card and so on, and there'll be his keys and his wedding ring and watch. I'd be obliged—and if you could tell me when I can—you know—have the body, for the funeral."

Feinman called the morgue and presently put the phone down looking disgusted. "I don't suppose it's anybody's fault, and it doesn't matter a damn to us—just academic—but that's damned annoying. No wallet, no money, no ring or watch or keys. So he was stabbed and robbed. For probably not more than ten bucks. And there's nothing to do about it. Even if we'd got on it right then, a million to one there'd have been any evidence at the scene, it was raining like hell."

"All you can do is write a report and shove it in Pending," said Maddox.

There wasn't anything in from the lab on Margaret Peller. Those boys took their time; but they'd be busy.

Feinman sat down at his typewriter, swearing, with the autopsy report. A tall thin man appeared in the doorway and asked, "Is this the detective office?"

"Yes, sir, what can we do for you? This is Sergeant Maddox —I'm Rodriguez." D'Arcy came in, late, as the newcomer entered.

He ducked his head in a correct little bow to all of them. He sat down in the offered chair. He was about forty, very well dressed in an expensive dark suit, snowy white shirt, silk tie. "Mr.—" said Maddox.

"Adler. Fritz Adler, sir. I am a German citizen, I represent my firm in this country—I do the buying. Ladies' high fashions. I am here twice a year on a buying trip. Naturally I stay at hotels—New York, San Francisco—I am now at the Beverly Hilton here—and also naturally I am not busy at my job all day. I go out to restaurants, sometimes the theater—like so." He gave them an apologetic smile. "Gentlemen, I am feeling like the fool over this thing, at first I think do not bother, the police will laugh—and then I think, better to tell you, I may not be the first."

"Yes, sir?" said Maddox. "What happened?"

"So, last night, I have not much to do, and after I had written some business letters in my room I go out, take a cab up to town, perhaps I find a film to see. But nothing attracts me, so I go into a bar, think to have a drink, and then go back to the hotel."

Maddox met D'Arcy's eye and said resignedly, "Yes, sir. Which one?"

"Eh? Oh, it is called Nikki's. A nice, elegant place on Hollywood Boulevard, clean, bright. We are," said Adler, "men of the world, eh? I am away from home, am I not? There is this" —he gestured graphically—"oh, but *Himmel*, quite the dish as you say! And complaisant. She sits beside me, we talk. I size her up immediately, it will not be cheap, but possibly worth it. You take me, gentlemen?"

"Blond?" asked Rodriguez without a smile.

"Oh, but no—very dark. One finds this unexpected beauty in mixed races—a purity of feature quite Greek. Part black, I think, part Spanish? Her name she told me is Juanita, that is Spanish."

"Where did she take you, the parking lot, around a dark corner?"

He looked from Maddox to Rodriguez. "Already you know this one? She says she has a car nearby, we go to her place. Yes, it was dark—up the side street. And *Gott*, I am never so surprised in my life, she reaches for her keys I think and it is a gun! You know her?"

"Not as intimately as we'd like to," said Maddox. "How much did she get?"

Adler sighed. "Two hundred and forty-three dollars, my Longines watch. Also a ruby ring."

"Not a bad night's haul. We'd like you to make a statement, sir." And there'd be another report to write.

Maddox was still typing up the statement for Adler to sign when the Van Nuys station called. One of their squad cars had just picked up Rex Slaney, spotted his car outside a motel. "*Gracias*," said Rodriguez. "There'll be somebody out to get him right away." He and D'Arcy started out together.

"I thought the weather report was wrong as usual," said D'Arcy, getting into the Dodge, "but I'll be damned if it doesn't look like rain again."

It had started to sprinkle very slightly by the time they got out to Van Nuys. The desk sergeant handed over Slaney, who was wearing a pair of cuffs and looked ready to chew nails. He matched the description from the nurse—big and burly, sandy hair long and scraggly.

"What about all my stuff at the motel? I'm only paid up today. Can I get it?"

"You're allowed one phone call," said Rodriguez. "Suppose you ask Mrs. Thomas to store it for you." They'd both seen the autopsy report on Peggy, and weren't feeling much like humoring him.

Back at Wilcox Street, they read him his rights and he said he understood them, but that was all they heard from him for a while. After a lot of play-acting, D'Arcy talking soft and Rodriguez tough, he seemed to get tired of the whole thing and said, "Oh, hell, lay off and take me to jail, you got to. I never meant to hurt the kid, but she was a goddamn nuisance,

whinin' around alla time, making messes, cryin' or getting sick
—but I never meant to hurt her, I guess you can say I just
don't know my own strength." He shrugged. Rodriguez
shrugged back and stood up.

"So come on."

"And leave me tell you something else too—Candy was always slappin' the kid around too, it wasn't just me. A kid's a
damn drag, I'll never take up with any chick has a kid
again—"

"I hope you won't have the chance for a while," said
D'Arcy. They told Whitwell to start the machinery on the
warrant. They hadn't had a chance to talk to the D.A.'s office
about it, but hopefully they asked for Murder Two. Neither of
them would take a bet it didn't get reduced to involuntary
manslaughter.

Sue sat debating with herself, alone in the little office, and
looked with disfavor at the first two lines of another report on
Pauline. She missed Daisy to talk things over with. And she
was feeling apprehensive about Pauline.

They had, of course, had the Stranges calling in four and
five time a day, and there just wasn't anything to tell them.
On the one hand, she'd rather liked Bill Blackwell's conclu-
sion, but now that was out the window too. She had talked to
Brenda Hansen about an hour ago at Hollywood High.
Brenda, an insolent-eyed too buxom hussy with false eye-
lashes, had said, "Pauline Strange? Who the hell's she?" and
with difficulty remembered when Sue prodded her. Certainly
Pauline hadn't been with Brenda in Acapulco.

It was, on the face of it, such a funny little tale. The girl
dropped off at home, last seen unlocking the door. Half an
hour later when the parents got home, no Pauline. No sign of
struggle or violence in the house, nothing missing. The neighbors hadn't seen or heard anything. Pauline didn't have a
driver's license, and there'd been nothing for her to drive anyway, the parents had the family car. And that was Thursday
night, three and a half days ago.

She put out her cigarette and got up to see if Ivor or another of the brains was in, to kick it around a little. As she came out a couple of citizens had just arrived on the landing.

"The sergeant at the desk said to come up and ask for Mrs. Maddox?" said the woman doubtfully.

"Yes, that's me—won't you come in and sit down? What can we do for you?"

"A police*woman*," said the woman. "I don't know—I don't mean to imply anything, but I'd just rather—now don't call me old-fashioned, Leo."

"Not about to say anything," said the man stolidly. "All I know is we want to talk to police period, and I understand the police here are pretty good, male or female I suppose."

Sue, no libber, suppressed amused sympathy. "We like to think so," she said, and glanced into the detective office. Her spouse was sprawled back in his desk chair, alone in the big room, talking on the phone, and she frowned at him disapprovingly. The citizens were evidently not locals; and at the moment Maddox didn't present a very good advertisement for the general quality of the L.A.P.D. His tie was pulled loose and his shirt unbuttoned to show part of the matt of chest hair; he had been running fingers through his black hair until a lock fell untidily across his forehead, and as Sue ushered in the citizens he was saying forcefully, "You can shove that! For Christ's sake, when are you goddamn ivory-tower nuts going to grow a little common sense? This obscenity of a worthless punk has beaten a three-year-old to death, and however the hell you read the law we see it as Murder Two." He looked up at Sue's frown. "All right, all right, but that's our view. We'll appreciate knowing how you decide it." He banged down the phone.

"This is Sergeant Maddox," said Sue formally.

The citizens seemed to be too intent on their own affairs to pick up the implication. "We're Mr. and Mrs. Leo Foster," said the man.

"Sit down. What can we—"

"Merciful heavens!" said Mrs. Foster crossly. "All this cross talk—wasting time. I'm sorry, but we've got to *do* something. Leo, had you better tell it or shall I?"

"You go ahead, Myra. You've got a head for getting facts organized, I'm only good at figures. Besides, I'm too mad at that damn doctor to talk straight."

"All *right*," she said. They sat down between Maddox' desk and D'Arcy's; Sue perched herself on D'Arcy's desk chair and found a memo pad for possible notes. The Fosters looked to be in their late forties. He was middle-sized, a little paunchy, with a square bulldog face, a bald dome, steady blue eyes. She was small and thin and energetic, with a long nose and snapping black eyes, pepper-and-salt hair. They were both well dressed. And they were both very worried, grim, and angry.

"All right," said Myra Foster. "I'll try to tell it as short as possible, not to waste any time and because we've got to *do* something. We live in Oak Park, Illinois. Leo's got his own insurance business. I've got just one relative left, my Aunt Helen —Helen Vickers, my mother's youngest sister. She lives—lived —lives here, she owns a house on LaClede Street. We've always written back and forth regular—we're pretty close—she lived with us when I was growing up. In fact, Leo and I'd like her to come back and live with us now. Our two girls are both married and away, and Aunt Helen's all alone, her husband died two years ago and they never had any children. She's sixty-six, and talk about having all your faculties, she's sharp as they come and her memory's better than mine. Am I going too fast?"

"No—go on." Maddox lit a cigarette.

"Well, she hadn't made up her mind to come back to us, on account of the climate. We were planning to come out here in November, and I hoped to persuade her then. And then the second week of August, Leo tripped over a ladder and broke his ankle. Which has something to do with it, I do assure you," said Myra Foster. "Because it was still in the cast and him on crutches two and a half weeks ago when this Mrs. Wilde called me long distance. I just knew her name. That neighborhood, when Aunt Helen and Uncle John first moved there, bought the house, most people owned their homes, neighbors knew each other, but it's changed. Apartments going up, people renting houses. Anyway, this Mrs. Wilde lives next door to Aunt Helen but she doesn't know her well, they haven't lived there long. And she called to tell me Aunt Helen'd broken her hip. Fell down the front steps, the cat got under her feet. And before the ambulance came Aunt Helen asked her to call me. Using Aunt Helen's phone, of course. I'm sorry to take so long to tell you, but you've got to have all the facts."

"Yes. And?" Maddox put out his cigarette. Sue's mind was half on Pauline.

"Well, I was wild. Leo couldn't go anywhere, and I couldn't leave him. Mrs. Wilde said it was the General hospital. I did know Aunt Helen's regular doctor, Dr. Collins, of course I didn't know his address but by the grace of God I remembered his name, Alonzo, and I got it from Information and wired him. I asked him to wire back how she was, but he never answered at all. I tell you, it was a nightmare. I called Information and got Mrs. Wilde's number, but she didn't know anything, all she told me was that she was feeding the cat. And then I got a post card from Aunt Helen." She opened her fat black bag and produced it, and Maddox looked at it with somnolent interest. The writing, a few terse lines, was square and distinctive. "Just as you see, she was in the hospital, the General hospital here. She asked the nurse to get the post card and mail it for her. They were going to operate and put in a pin, the way they do, and then the doctor said she'd have to be in a convalescent home awhile, but—well, you can see for yourself, Aunt Helen's not one to give up easy, she felt she'd be home again in a few weeks and getting around fine."

"Yes," said Maddox patiently.

"Well, that set my mind a little at rest but naturally I was worried. I wrote her at the hospital, I expected she'd write me back when she could, get a nurse to send another card at least, to tell me about the convalescent home and where she'd be, but I didn't get a word. And then last week"—she opened the bag again—"I got every single one of my letters and cards back from the post office, all marked ADDRESSEE UNKNOWN."

"Oh, really?" Maddox sat up. Feinman had come in and was sitting smoking quietly, listening.

Leo Foster, sitting back with hands clasped over his paunch, suddenly uttered a slight chuckle. "If I know Helen," he said, "wherever she is, she's putting up a fight. But you can imagine how we felt."

"I was *wild*," said Myra Foster. "You can imagine! And Aunt Helen hadn't mentioned the name of the doctor at the hospital—and then I called the other doctor long distance and he was out of town. We couldn't find out a thing! I called the General hospital and just got the run-around—I know in a big place like that there's red tape, but nobody seemed to know a thing. They just said they never did forward mail for patients. And I said to Leo, we've got to go and find out. So as soon as he was out of the cast, last Thursday, we made arrangements. We flew out on Saturday. We went right to Aunt Helen's house, I had a key, she's very businesslike about things and she always said suppose she should die suddenly—" Abruptly Myra Foster gave a loud sob, and said, "Excuse me —that doesn't do any good, but I'm so worried! And *that doctor!* You wouldn't believe the run-around we had! Mrs. Wilde didn't know a thing, of course. I ought to say, of course Aunt Helen has friends here, but not such close ones the last couple of years—the Bennetts moved away when she retired, and Clara Dow went back East to her son when she lost her husband and the Kruppners were both killed in that awful plane crash—there was Mrs. James, but she had a stroke last year and can't get around, I'd called her the first thing but she didn't even know about Aunt Helen breaking her hip. She hasn't heard from her or anything about it, and she's worried sick too." Myra took a breath. "Well! We went down to the hospital and we just kept asking, until they finally gave us some answers. Finally looked up their records. Aunt Helen had been there, up to ten days ago. She was operated on by this Dr. Brokaw. He wasn't at the hospital then, but we got his office address. He wasn't at the office—that snippy nurse, I don't think she bothered to take in half what we told her—she wouldn't call his emergency number, just said we'd have to make an appointment. We went to see Aunt Helen's regular doctor, he's back now, but all he said was that he hadn't seen her, he doesn't do surgery like that, and this Dr. Brokaw had a good reputation. We went back to the hospital yesterday, we got another run-around from all those nurses, I thought there had to be some record of where she'd been moved, but all they could find was the record for an ambulance when she left the hospital, that was then on the eighteenth, ten days back. The doctor'd made arrangements, they said. They finally paged him, and that time we saw him. I can't say I liked him much, and he gave us another run-around. We had to realize how many patients he saw every day, he'd have to look up records at his office, he couldn't spare any time now, and so on. Well, we were waiting this morning when his office opened, and his nurse looked up the record— It's not natural the way they do things now!" said Myra fiercely. "Not knowing people's names—just records in a file cabinet—but anyway, it said that she'd been taken to this convalescent home, the Sunnyvale Convalescent Home on Vermont Avenue. I should say we've rented a car—Leo says I'm organized but I guess I'm upset, *and* with good reason. We drove right there and asked to see Aunt Helen. And" —she sat up straighter in the chair and her eyes were blazing— "it was a terrible place—smelly and dirty, just an old house really—this nurse, or she was dressed like a nurse, she took us to a room and said she was there—and it wasn't Aunt Helen at all! A fat old woman, practically senile, I'd never seen before—and I looked, and she had a little bracelet on that said HELEN VICKERS on it, but it wasn't Aunt Helen!"

"You don't tell me," said Maddox, looking interested.

"And when I said so, this nurse got all flustered, and said it wasn't regular visiting hours anyway, but you can bet we weren't putting up with another run-around, and Leo spoke his mind and demanded to see the manager or head nurse or whoever was in charge, and this other woman showed up, I don't know her name, and tried to make out we didn't know what we were talking about—I could have hit her—but it was the other way around, all of a sudden there were two men there, two big fellows, orderlies I guess, and they just bundled us out the front door and locked it—"

"Now you don't tell me," said Maddox, sitting up.

"And about then," said Foster, "I thought it was time to go to the police. I don't know why anybody'd want to kidnap Helen, she's only got John's savings and her Social Security, but that place isn't fit for man or beast, the little we saw, and if she's there we want her out of it."

CHAPTER 4

"Whatever the ins and outs," said Maddox, "it seems to me you need some official back-up here. That's the queerest story I've heard in a while." He stood up.

"You're quick off the mark," said Foster approvingly. "That's what I hoped you'd say—what the hell are these people up to, but anyway, they can't throw the police out." He got up too.

"Then let's *go*," said Myra fiercely. "If Aunt Helen is in that place—"

Maddox introduced them to Feinman on the way out. Sue, wondering about Aunt Helen, went back to her report on Pauline.

They all got into Feinman's Chevy. The Fosters were silent on the ride up to Vermont Avenue. When Feinman spotted the address, he said, "That's a convalescent home?"

"What I said when we saw it first," said Foster.

Here and there around the county there were some relics like this one still standing, the Victorian mansions ninety and a hundred years old. Incongruously this one sat, back from the street, alone; Vermont was all business, shops and garages and office buildings, built flush to the sidewalk, and one narrow oasis between two block units held the old three-story house, tall and thin, minus its gingerbread but looking ready to fall down, unpainted for years, several upper windows boarded up. There was no attempt at landscaping around it, bare packed dirt in front, a rutted driveway; several cars were parked at random in the front yard.

Maddox and Feinman led the way up to the high front porch, the Fosters behind. The door was locked; there wasn't any sign anywhere identifying the place as a convalescent home. Maddox knocked loudly on the door, and kept on knocking for three minutes before the door was opened a crack by a thin dark girl in a white uniform. They both had their badges out. "Police—let us in. We'd like to see whoever's in charge here."

She backed away looking frightened, stammering in Spanish. "Meesus Parks—I get—"

"That's her!" said Myra Foster. "That other one! Now then, you won't get rid of us so easy this time, my lady! I'll see if my aunt's here or know the reason why—"

The woman who had appeared at the back of the entrance hall was galvanized into action and words. She came gushing to meet them, ignoring Maddox and Feinman. "But I'm so glad you've come back, Mrs.—I'm sorry, I didn't catch your name—it's all just an unfortunate misunderstanding, I'm so terribly sorry such a thing happened—really I was so upset when you, er, let us know about it I didn't know what I was doing—I've been in touch with the hospital, and I can assure you—" She was a tall thin angular woman in starched white uniform, nurse's cap on lank dark hair; she had an ugly bucktoothed smile, and her voice was obsequious.

Maddox shoved the badge under her nose. "Mrs. Vickers," he said. "Is she here? We can get a search warrant if we have to."

The smile and voice faltered. "Police—" she said, her head jerked back unvoluntarily; for a split second she gave an uncanny impression of a snake reared back to strike. "I didn't—but that's just what I was trying to explain—a very unfortunate mistake—I'm expecting a call about the matter at any minute—"

"If we have to search this place room by room—" said Myra Foster, and marched determinedly toward the closed double doors to the left. The place hadn't been remodeled inside; there was no reception desk, no office, only the original square entry, double doors right and left, a cross hall up beyond. The bare wooden floor was dusty and littered with fluffs and miscellany, and there were cobwebs festooned from the tall ceiling.

"Please! No—I'm trying to tell you, Mrs. Vickers isn't here—please, I'm expecting a call—"

Myra threw the doors open. It was the original old double parlor of the house, at least sixty by thirty, and now it was crowded with human flotsam: old people, twenty-eight or thirty of them, some in wheelchairs, some just sitting on sagging old chairs, sofas—all sorts of old people, in various states of dress and undress. A TV was blaring in one corner; no one seemed to be watching it. Permeating the whole house, Maddox was gradually aware, was a pervasive stench—of illness, of unwashed bodies, of human waste, of steamy institutional cooking.

Nearest the doors an old man was tied into a wheelchair; he appeared to be naked except for an old wool bathrobe much stained. His gray face showed a thick stubble of beard, and his eyes were vague, but at the sound of strange voices he seemed to rouse, struggled in the chair. "Help," he mumbled, "help me—"

"Please! Visitors aren't allowed—I told you she's not here—" A phone rang somewhere and Mrs. Parks uttered a gasp of relief and scuttled up the hall.

"I told you, a terrible place!" said Myra Foster. "None of these people are being cared for properly—it's disgraceful."

"What do we do, search the whole house?" Feinman's nose wrinkled.

"And then notify the Board of Health," said Maddox. But Mrs. Parks was scuttling back down the hall.

"A terrible mistake," she panted at them. "I don't know when such a thing has ever happened, we're just all awfully, awfully sorry, Mrs. Uh—know how it must look to you, but you've got to realize, it's so hard to keep help in a place like this, we're always shorthanded—we do our best, but it's difficult—so many of the poor old people quite incontinent, you know—I do hope you won't make any trouble over it, just a terrible mistake—I've just heard from Mrs. Cleveland and it's quite all right, Mrs. Vickers is there and always has been, and you're quite welcome to—"

"Where?" asked Feinman bluntly.

"At the other home—this is just a branch actually," said Mrs. Parks brightly. "I just can't understand such a dreadful, er, mix-up happening, but apparently they were transferred from the hospital at the same time—Miss Runnels and Mrs.

Vickers—and there was just some little mix-up with the ambulance. But it's quite all right now we know—this is the address, you'll find her there, so you see it's all right—" She was edging them toward the door.

Maddox said interestedly, "Do you get your patients mixed up often?"

"I said I don't know when such a thing has happened—"

"When was this place inspected last?"

"Last month," she snapped. "Really, I assure you—" The toothy smile flickered.

"I never heard of such a thing!" said Myra indignantly. "How could there be a mistake like that? My aunt's got a tongue in her head, and she knows who she is!"

"Sort it out later—let's go see if she is at this other place," said Foster.

"You'll find it's quite all right," said Mrs. Parks.

"Help," muttered the man in the wheelchair. "Home—don't belong—help—" Mrs. Parks closed the double doors with a little click.

Maddox surveyed her coldly. "Oh, for heaven's sake let's go!" said Myra. "The important thing's Aunt Helen."

"That," said Feinman in the car, "looks pretty gamey to me. Unless the health inspector's taking graft."

"We'll report it and try to find out. Something else funny—two Sunnyvale rest homes? A branch, the lady says."

The second one was on Hillhurst, and presented a smart brick and stucco front with double glass doors, shiningly polished, into a spankingly hygienic-looking lobby. There was a reception counter along one side with a fresh-looking blonde in white uniform behind it. An old lady sat knitting on one of the vinyl-covered couches, and gave them a curious stare. There were bunches of fresh flowers all around the lobby.

"Yes, can I help you?" asked the blonde, smiling.

Forestalling Myra, Maddox said, "We'd like to see Mrs. Vickers. Did Mrs. Parks call?"

The smile vanished momentarily. "Oh—about that. I'll get Mrs. Cleveland. She said someone would be coming." She pushed buttons, spoke into an intercom, and almost immediately an older woman came out of the office at the other side of the lobby.

"You're the relatives," she said with a friendly smile, advancing. "Mrs.—"

"Mr. and Mrs. Foster. I don't understand any of this at all—"

Maddox had the badge out. "It does seem to be a little bit irregular," he said softly.

"Police—oh, there was hardly any necessity for that, was there? Oh, I quite understand that you were upset, Mrs. Foster. I'm Mrs. Cleveland, by the way, I'm the head nurse here." She was a handsome piece of goods; she couldn't be over thirty-five, tall and graceful, with dark hair in a becoming smooth pompadour, regular features, a magnificent milky complexion, ice-blue eyes. She gave a little laugh. "It's dreadfully embarrassing for us, I'm afraid—it looks so inefficient, but I don't recall such a thing ever happening before."

"What did happen?" asked Maddox.

"Why, it seems that Miss Runnels and Mrs. Vickers left the General hospital the same day, and possibly the ambulance attendants were confused—at any rate, it's straightened out now, and I hope you won't feel—"

"I want to see her," said Myra impatiently.

"Yes, of course." She looked only slightly disconcerted when all four of them moved after her, but didn't object. "I'm afraid, Mrs. Foster, you may find her greatly aged." This was a modern, efficiently designed building; the tiled corridor was spotless, and they had glimpses into bright, clean, cheerful rooms, some with two beds, some with four, all with windows looking out on a central patio where greenery showed. They passed an occasional patient in a wheelchair, one stout old woman proceeding slowly, pushing a steel walker.

"What do you mean? Just a broken hip wouldn't—"

"Any accident brings the risk of shock, you know, and sometimes elderly people go downhill quite rapidly. I only wanted to prepare you—" She stood back, pushing a swing door open, and the Fosters surged in.

"Aunt Helen—thank goodness, it *is* her—but she looks— Aunt Helen?" There were two beds in this room, but only one was occupied. The old lady lying flat and still in it looked thin and white and peaceful. Her gray hair was plastered smoothly down to her skull, freshly combed, and she was clean and neat in a fresh hospital gown. But she breathed slowly, deeply, and her eyes didn't open.

"She had rather a restless night," said Mrs. Cleveland, "and said she was in pain, so I authorized a hypo only an hour ago. It may be some time before she's awake."

Maddox bent over the thin figure and gently pulled back one eyelid. "Are you a doctor, sir?" she asked sharply.

He met her eyes and opened his mouth, but Myra the energetic got in ahead of him. "I can't make head or tail of this whole rigmarole, and I must say this place looks perfectly all right, but nevertheless whatever did happen happened here, and I'll feel better if I just take her some place else. Right now."

"The doctor will have to authorize—"

"We're not quite that regimented yet, Mrs. Cleveland," said Maddox mildly. "Mrs. Foster is Mrs. Vickers' nearest relative and prepared to take the responsibility."

"I certainly am! I don't know what to say—" She looked at Maddox. "But I'd like her own doctor to see her, Dr. Collins, she's gone to him for years and she likes him—and there must be other places—"

"That's a good idea," said Maddox easily. "I'll arrange things."

"You may use the phone in my office," said Mrs. Cleveland frigidly.

"Oh, I won't impose on you." He gave her an amiable smile and went back to the lobby, where there was a booth. He made sure the door was shut before he dialed the Emergency desk at the receiving hospital and ordered an ambulance. He didn't have to suggest that Myra Foster stay with her aunt until it arrived. He and Feinman went outside to wait for it.

"Now what in hell is behind all that?" asked Feinman, lighting a cigarette.

"Funny setup. It looks to me as if it was just a piece of idiotic carelessness, Joe—leading on to something else maybe. Didn't our Myra say, not natural, all just records in a file cabinet—and she was a new patient to the doctor, to everybody at the General. The names got switched somehow."

"How could they get switched, when this old girl's supposed to have all her buttons?"

"That's what I'm wondering about," said Maddox, his nose twitching thoughtfully. "This looks like a very nice place, Joe —for a rest home. And even nurses and doctors make honest mistakes—and if they're honest, admit it. But one thing I'd take a bet on—that hypo had morphine in it, and maybe double the usual dose."

Daisy came back about noon, annoyed, and said after sitting through all the divorces, the judge had adjourned for an hour and then granted the defense attorney a postponement to locate a missing witness. "God knows when it'll go to trial now."

"Well, I'm glad to see you anyway. This thing about Pauline—"

Daisy listened, agreed, and said again they'd done all they could with a missing report out. D'Arcy and Rodriguez came up the stairs grumbling about the weather; it had settled down to a steady rain again. "I'm ready for lunch," said Daisy. "How about you?"

They'd just collected their coats and bags to go out when D'Arcy looked in. "We'll want one of you on this. Rape call just in." He and Rodriguez were shrugging into their coats again.

"For heaven's sake," said Sue, annoyed. "All right, I'd like to lose a few pounds anyway. Where is it?"

"The hospital."

In the lobby of Emergency at the receiving hospital, Patrolman Ben Loth was waiting for them. "One thing about this job," he said, "you never know what you're going to run into next. I'm just cruising along down on Westminster, one end of the beat, and all of a sudden this girl comes busting out of an apartment like a bat out of hell, naked as a jaybird—she had a coat but she hadn't put it on yet—and goes running down the street, so I take off after her. By the time I got the siren on, she's half into the coat, and when she hears me she turns around and makes for the squad, right out in the street, I just had time to brake, thought I'd hit her. She says she's been kidnaped and raped, she knows the guy's name, he lives at that apartment. So I figured, get her to the hospital first."

"Join the force and see life," said Rodriguez. "Where is she?"

"The doctor's got her in a treatment room now."

"Well, you'd better get back on tour."

"Sure. Hope she'll be O.K.," said Loth. "She's a good-looker, seems like a nice girl."

Five minutes later the doctor came out, not Hirschner, a darker, older man looking slightly amused. "Suppose you want to talk to her. She's all right—she was raped and mauled around a little, but no permanent damage. She's over being scared and getting mad, which is a good sign."

Sue went in alone but in a minute poked her head out and said, "She's not shy. She wants us all to hear about it. Her name's Dolores Mulvaney."

"Honestly, I appreciate your sending a policewoman," said the girl as soon as they came in. "But I don't mind as long as I've got something *on*." She blushed. "How that *sounds*—but you feel sort of helpless without any clothes. That nurse was so nice, gave me one of her uniforms and even a slip, to get home in." She was sitting, clad in the uniform, on the edge of the examining table. "Believe me, it'll be a long time before I try to be nice and kind to somebody again! And believe me, I've been thinking twice about what Mother says, too. I mean, all this equality bit, but"—she looked rueful—"I guess there are still some things girls shouldn't do."

"You told the patrolman you know the man who raped you?" asked D'Arcy.

"Well, in a *way*. This was last night—gah, it feels like a million years! My car's in the garage, it needed a new radiator, so I had to take the bus to work and everywhere, it's a nuisance. I was supposed to get it back today." She kept brushing back her long dark hair; she was a pretty girl, just into her twenties. "When it stopped raining yesterday I went out, just to be going some place after being cooped up in the apartment, you know? I took the bus up to Hollywood Boulevard and window-shopped some, and then I thought I'd eat out before I went home."

"You live alone, Miss Mulvaney?"

"Yes, I'm from Fresno, all the family lives there but I wanted to try it on my own here, I work at Columbia Records, in the office, I've got an apartment down on Normandie."

"O.K., so then what?"

"Well, I went into this restaurant, it looked nice, I'd never been there before. The London Grill, right on the Boulevard. Only when I got in it looked kind of expensive, so I didn't go into the dining room, I just sat at the counter up in front, I thought that'd probably be cheaper. And while I was waiting and having some coffee, the man next to me asked for the sugar and we just got talking. Casual, you know. And haven't I laughed at Mother when she says don't talk to strange men! Hah! Look—" She appealed to Sue. "You can *tell*—it's not like a hundred years ago when you had to be introduced by a relative or something before you said two words to anybody. It was just being friendly—and something came up about my car, and he said the bus service was so awful, and could he drive me home. Oh, he'd said his name was Williams. I didn't especially want to take him up on that, but he was perfectly polite, and then he said he had to pick up his wife first, so that *sounded* all right—and besides—and besides—"

"What?" asked Sue.

"Oh, I know now I was a damned fool," said Dolores miserably, "but you hear so much about it these days, it seems everybody's hipped on it—I didn't want to offend him. I thought if I said no, he'd think right off it was because he was black—and he was terribly polite, and said about his wife—"

D'Arcy sighed and shifted, leaning on the sterile cabinet. "So you got in his car."

"Yes. And right away I knew I shouldn't have. He started down La Brea, and he never mentioned his wife again, and when we got to Third I said we were past where I lived, but the next thing I knew he'd turned onto a side street and stopped the car and grabbed at me. I tried to fight him, and I know you're supposed to scream but I couldn't get one out, and then he hit me and I guess knocked me out. When I came to he was dragging me up some stairs, and I saw the number on the door right at the top there, eleven, and then he opened it and sort of threw me in. I don't think there was anybody in the street to see, it was after dark then. I was in that apartment all night," she said solemnly. "I've never been so scared in my life. There was a girl there too—another white girl."

"What?" said Rodriguez.

"He called her Betsy. She was as scared of him as I was, I

think, but she did whatever he told her. She—she had to watch while he—you know—was raping me, and all. And when he finally went to bed, about the middle of the night, he said if she let me go he'd cut her heart out— I begged and begged her, but she tied me to a chair. And this morning he did it to me again—they'd taken all my clothes, all but my coat, that was on the end of the couch, and I was watching for any chance—even if I had to run out naked, if I could just get away! And he went into the kitchen just for a minute while she was in the bathroom, and I just grabbed my coat and I thought I'd never get the door open but I did, and I practically fell down the stairs—and I was never so glad to see a police car in my life! He was such a nice officer, too—"

"We'd like a description of both of them," said Rodriguez.

"You can't miss *him*. He's over six feet and awfully big, and pretty black. He's got a mustache. She's bigger than me but not much, I don't think very old, and she's got sort of pale red hair."

"Well, suppose I see that you get home all right," said Sue, "and we'll hope the detectives can pick them up."

"You're awfully kind," said Dolores. "Thanks. I had to leave my bag there with my keys but the manager'll let me in." She heaved a deep sigh. "I'm starving, and I guess I'll sleep for a week."

There wasn't much chance that Williams or the other girl would still be at that apartment, but the neighbors might know something about them, or the manager if there was one on the premises. Sue had driven her own car, and took the girl off. D'Arcy and Rodriguez drove down to Westminster Place to the address where Loth had spotted the girl.

It was one of the old rundown apartment houses in that part of town, which was increasingly these days beginning to consist of mixed neighborhoods, the Negroes moving uptown. There would be about thirty units in this one, three stories. D'Arcy left the Dodge in a red zone and they went in. There wasn't any door marked MANAGER, just numbers from one to ten on the ground floor. They climbed old wooden stairs. At the top, across the landing, was a door marked 11. And in the little name slot beside it was a dirty strip of paper with WILLIAMS on it.

"Such a stupid thing," said Rodriguez. "The louts get stupider all the time." He banged once on the door, just a futile gesture.

It opened promptly. Framed in the doorway was a plump young woman in a bedraggled cotton housecoat. Reddish-blond hair fell limp about her round face. "Oh, I don't believe it," said Rodriguez. "We're looking for Mr. Williams, is he here?"

She opened the door wider and stepped back almost indifferently, and they went into a shabby living room nearly bare of furniture. A big black fellow was sitting on the couch drinking from a can of beer.

They both showed him the badges. "We've got some questions to ask you about a rape," said Rodriguez.

"I don't know anything about a rape. I been right here."

"We know you have. You're coming down to the station to think up some answers. You, too," D'Arcy added to the girl.

"I don't know what you're talking about," said Williams.

The girl said, "You leave him be," and made a weak effort to pull D'Arcy's arm.

"That's helpful," said Rodriguez. "Technically speaking, resisting—so we can legally look at anything out in the open." He made for the TV in the corner and picked up a handbag. It was a smart brown alligator bag; he opened it and looked at the contents.

"That's mine," said the girl.

"You really are a pair of stupids, aren't you?" said Rodriguez. "With Dolores Mulvaney's wallet here, driver's license, Social Security card, library card—right in plain sight—and she'll identify you both."

"I don't know what you're talking about," said Williams.

"Oh, come on," said Rodriguez. "You go get dressed, Betsy, and make it snappy."

It was pouring again by the time Maddox and Feinman got back to the office at four o'clock. They found D'Arcy and Rodriguez questioning a big black man and looking as if they weren't getting much, and Daisy talking to a sullen-eyed girl. "Something new gone down?" said Maddox.

They welcomed the excuse for a break, and told them about the rape. "I don't know why you're trying to get answers out of him," said Rodriguez. "The girl will identify, and there's plenty of evidence. It couldn't be much stupider. It's so stupid it's silly."

"You might as well book them in and write a report," agreed Feinman.

Maddox sat down at his desk and rubbed his stubbled jaw. "And where've you been?" asked Rodriguez.

"I wish I knew," said Maddox absently. "See if you have any bright ideas on it," and he told them, at some length, about Aunt Helen.

"Oh, I like that," said Rodriguez, pleased with something *outré*. "But I don't see what could be behind it, unless it was just a great big goof by the omnipotent hospital, and all the pros are covering up for each other. If any of us poor peasants ever got to suspecting that doctors and nurses are human too —It reminds me of something, what?" He ruminated. "I know. That Paris Exhibition story. Girl and mother check into a hotel, mother ill, girl out to find doctor, when she comes back, presto, no mother—hotel room different color, different wall-paper, mother's luggage gone, everybody swears she checked in alone, never was a mother—"

"Because the mother was carrying plague and they were afraid of scaring off the tourist trade, yes," said Maddox. "Well, Aunt Helen's tucked up comfortably in bed with Myra in attendance, her own doctor's coming to see her, and the doctor at Emergency thinks she'll be all right. Fuller report to-morrow, and I hope she can talk to us sometime. I'm inclined to agree with you, César—just a great big goof—but there's still something funny about it. And that first place has got to be reported to the Board of Health. They'll probably close it up *pronto*. Those boys are so hot on hygiene. I'd better do that." He pulled the phone forward.

"Oh, there was a lab report," said D'Arcy. "Just before you came in. It's on your desk."

Maddox found it and started to read it. "Well, better late than never." There had been, as Dabney said, hundreds of latent prints in Margaret Peller's house, not all worth lifting or identifiable, and most of them hers. But the lab had now identified two of them, and described them precisely. Found on side and front of refrigerator in the kitchen. On one of them the lab had pinpointed eleven matching marks, on the other, twelve; only ten were needed legally to match person with print. Therefore, the lab concluded that they were the prints of Randolph Simpson, who was in their records with a pedigree of burglary, one count, and felony drunk driving, one count. There was a valid address for him; he was on parole. "Do you feel like going out again, Joe?"

"Not much," said Feinman sleepily.

"Neither do I, but it seems we're fated to. Let me make that call." He talked to the Board of Health for some time, and then got up and picked up his raincoat.

"You really need me? Somebody ought to write a report on Aunt Helen."

"True. I hadn't got that far yet. All right, you do that then."

It was raining steadily, and very dark outside; he switched on the Maserati's headlights. They'd been due for an early wet winter, after a series of dry ones, but this was a little too much of a good thing.

The address for Randolph Simpson was Madera Avenue in the Atwater district. As he looked for street names Maddox reflected that he wasn't far from Aunt Helen's house here, on LaClede, and on impulse passed Madera and went on there to have a look at it. It was a nice-looking little house, reminding him of Anton Czerny's house—outside: a neat frame bungalow painted white with yellow trim, the strip of lawn in front green. On the deep front porch, motionless as a statue, sat a large and dignified black cat, staring into the silver spikes of the rain. Aunt Helen's cat? He hoped absently that the uncaring Mrs. Wilde was still feeding it; no, the Fosters were staying here now; but the cat didn't look worried about anything.

He went around the block and drove back to Madera. That address was a new apartment building. He couldn't get an answer at the apartment he wanted, and tried the manageress downstairs.

"Oh, Mr. Simpson. He was lucky to get a job a couple of weeks ago, he'd been out of work awhile. Sure, I know where —he told me about it when he paid up the back rent. It's an appliance repair place, Bill's Certified Service, on Western."

Maddox found a phone booth up on Glendale Boulevard and looked up the address. As he headed back for Hollywood a rather spectacular thunderstorm was going on, and—goofing off—he pulled up alongside the curb to enjoy it. He always got a kick out of a good thunder and lightning display. So did Sue. They didn't occur often in this climate, and he hoped Sue was somewhere where she could enjoy it properly.

When he got to Bill's Certified Service it was after five; this would be his last stop of the day, unless Simpson looked so good for the homicide he decided to take him in for questioning. In which case he'd be doing some overtime.

It was a small, dirty, cluttered front office, with a good deal of noise from a much larger place behind. Maddox explained his business to the fat bald man who had appeared as the door opened. "Simpson? Yeah, he's here. Hey, Ranny! You're a cop? Don't tell me you think Ranny's done something? He wouldn't. Yeah, I know he's on P.A., I done a little time myself once and a good guy helped me get started all over, I like to pass it on—but I know how to size up a guy. Ranny really means to stay all square, he wouldn't've done nothing."

Simpson told him that all over, earnestly; he was a lanky, farmerish-looking fellow with a nervous Adam's apple. "Place on Poinsettia?" he said. "Seems that was an address I went to, fix an old refrigerator, last week sometime." They looked it up in the rudimentary records, and it was there. Last Tuesday. "See, we're kind of cut-rate, on account I don't have much overhead," said Bill. "People call us from all over town."

It wasn't likely that Simpson, a mile and a half away, had heard any rumors about Margaret Peller's reputed wealth, and a look inside the house wouldn't have led him to think it was worth burglarizing; but the L.A.P.D.'s reputation had been built partly on thoroughness, so Maddox asked Simpson about last Thursday afternoon. They should have an autopsy report tomorrow, but for pretty certain that had been the crucial time.

"Thursday, say noon to six," he said.

"Thursday. Oh, yeah," said Simpson, his brow clearing. "That was the day we had that old bitch in. We had to practically take it apart and fix everything, new motor, the works. I was right here all that afternoon, Bill can say."

"He was sure, and so was I. That was a hell of a job, and all for fifty-eight bucks. You satisfied?"

Maddox decided he had to be. The lab often handed them useful evidence; just now and then it led them astray. It was six o'clock. He drove straight home to Gregory Avenue. He left the Maserati in the street, there being no garage; as he passed the Patterson house three doors down he glanced at that garage, which Sue rented for the Chrysler, but the door was down and told him nothing.

The house was dark and silent. He switched on lights and the front-room heater; wandered into the second bedroom and contemplated his walls of books; he wondered where Sue was. Presently, feeling neglected, he made himself a drink.

Sue had got back to the station at two-thirty, after ferrying the nurse's clothes back to the hospital and stopping for a sandwich, and went right out again with Ellis on an attempted child molestation. The theory was that a sympathetic female officer would find it easier to talk to female or minor victims; sometimes it worked out. But in this case, the mother was hysterical and worked the child up to hysterics, and it took quite a while to extract any facts and a rudimentary description, which was probably useless. Sue was feeling annoyed with humanity when she got back to Wilcox Street, dripping and feeling hungry again, at four-thirty.

Of course Ellis said she could write the report on it.

Nobody else was in but Feinman. Presently she heard the phone ring across the hall, and a minute later Feinman came out grumbling to himself. "Damnation. This end of a day. I had to be a cop yet."

"Something new down," said Sue, looking up from her typewriter.

He was putting on his raincoat. "And my grandmother wanted me to be a rabbi. Sometimes I think I should've listened. Nice quiet contemplative life. Something new in spades. Squad car just spotted a body up off Mulholland. A girl in a red pantsuit. In all this damn rain. And—"

D'Arcy came upstairs taking off his coat.

"We'll want pictures, and Dabney's off and Rowan's out, and in all this rain what kind of evidence on the scene—"

"Pictures?" said D'Arcy. "New corpse? All right, I'm here, aren't I?" D'Arcy's hobby and passion was photography. He wasn't crazy about the official Speed Graphic, but he was efficient with it.

"Red pantsuit?" echoed Sue. Suddenly she heard Sylvia Nichols saying it again, she had on a coral pantsuit and black loafers— "A young girl, Joe?"

"What the man said."

"Wait a minute, I'll go along." Sue reached for her coat. "I don't know if I'm having a hunch, but I want to see."

With D'Arcy, encumbered with the big camera and floodlights, they drove up there in Feinman's car. It was starting to get dark. Mulholland Drive was up in the Hollywood hills above the city, residential blocks not far below, but up where the squad car waited it was all precipitous hillside above and below the winding road, wild undergrowth, sage and manzanita deep on the slopes.

The squad had its lights on. "Just chance I spotted it," said Patrolman Schultz as they came by. "I was by this spot every day but it could've been there a week, I don't know. But there was all this thunder and lightning—I get a kick out of a good thunderstorm—and I pulled up to watch the lightning, and this one bolt sizzled right down, like right in the gap between the hills—I know it didn't really, miles away, but it looked that way—and my eyes kind of followed it, and I saw this flash of red. So I climbed down partway and looked. You can hardly see it now."

It was raining solidly and Feinman said, "For God's sake be careful, Sue—" But they got down there, fifteen steep feet down the muddy hill, through wet undergrowth, and with the help of the headlights and the men's flashlights, they looked.

And Sue said flatly, "Well, you know it's got to be her. Pauline." By the description, size, coloring, clothes. Here was Pauline, her coral pantsuit sodden and dark with rain, lying sprawled grotesquely facedown, nearly hidden by the undergrowth. Dead since when? And how?

"You can't see a damn thing," said Feinman. "There won't be any evidence left anyway, all the rain—but she's limp. Ei-

ther it was in the last twelve hours or a long while before."
They all knew the rules about rigor mortis.

"Before," said Sue. "I think. Maybe last Thursday night."

They did what they could. D'Arcy took photographs, and
they called the morgue wagon. It was full dark then and the
rain streaming down: getting on toward seven o'clock. The
wagon collected the body and they went back to the station.

"The report can wait," said Feinman. "I'm going home."

"Yes, Ivor'll think I'm lost, strayed, or stolen. Damn," said
Sue. "Overtime. We'll have to call the Stranges—get the father
to identify her formally. But I know one thing I want to do
about this, we'll get on it in the morning—"

She got home at seven-thirty and told Maddox about it.
"What do we do for dinner?" he asked.

"Go out. I'm such a mess—have to do my hair again tonight, and I've torn both stockings and my shoes are all
muddy—give me five minutes to change and we'll go out
somewhere, I'm starving. But I'll tell you one thing I'm going
to do tomorrow—tackle Pauline's boy friend. Because that's
the logical place to start, and I don't think I buy his story alto-
gether."

CHAPTER 5

Both Mr. and Mrs. Strange came down to view the body, which was unfortunate. Even cleaned up roughly, the body wasn't a pleasant sight. There was a good deal of cyanotic darkening of the face where it had lain head-down for the blood to settle. Any conjecture about the cause of death would have to wait for an autopsy; she could have been strangled or beaten to death, there was too much post-mortem staining to say. The clothes had been sent to the lab downtown then, and the body was covered with a sheet on a cold tray.

"But she wouldn't be eighteen till December!" sobbed Mrs. Strange. "Why? What could have happened to her? She was a good girl—she wasn't wild, running around with the kind that use dope—"

"But she was home!" cried Strange almost wildly. "She was safe at home Thursday night—what in God's name happened?"

"She never," wailed Mrs. Strange, "had a date with any other boy than Bill—such a good reliable boy—"

And that, of course, was what was in Sue's mind, as she told Feinman on Tuesday morning. Now they had something definite to do about Pauline. "I only talked to a couple of her girl friends casually, but all we've heard from everybody is just that—she'd never looked at another male than the Blackwell boy. Well, not a boy—he's nineteen, and a big fellow. She left that house voluntarily, and he's one of the very few people she'd have left with, at that time of night."

"It is so often the nearest and dearest," conceded Feinman. "So we go lean on him and see what he says."

Bill Blackwell was attending Los Angeles City College; it

wasn't a prestige college, attracting mostly low-income stu-
dents with part-time jobs. Its campus sprawled along Vermont
Avenue on the east side of Hollywood. Sue let Feinman talk
to the registrar, who shied back at the badge; and they were
waiting outside the classroom when Blackwell showed up for
his first class, took him a few steps down the corridor away
from the crowd at the door.

"We've found Pauline," Sue told him.

He nodded silently. His pleasantly craggy face looked hag-
gard. "The Stranges called me last night. I didn't know what
to say. What to think. It just doesn't seem—anything that
could happen—to anybody you know. Let alone Pauline."

"We'd like to talk to you," said Feinman. "Is there a study
hall or somewhere?"

"I couldn't tell you a thing—" He glanced around a little
helplessly and said, "The student lounge, I guess," and led
them there, an impersonal rectangle of modern, square chairs
and tables, with great windows looking out on other college
buildings, on gravel paths and a few trees, flower beds.

"We'd like to know where you were on Thursday night,"
said Sue.

"Me? You aren't thinking I'd do anything to Pauline?" He
looked more bewildered than belligerent. "That's crazy. I
don't know anything about it."

"Thursday night," said Feinman. "You were out with her
the night before."

"Yes—I told you"—he looked at Sue—"she was just the
same as usual. Thursday night I went over to Bob Ledbetter's.
I had an exam coming up—"

"The term's just started," said Sue.

"That's right." He was talking in a dull tone, head bent.
"The Latin teacher gives an exam once a month, first-year
Latin—you can't get it in high school now, and I've been having
a struggle with it. It was a madhouse at home, the younger
kids, so I went over to Bob's. He had the same exam. I do that
two, three times a month. We've known each other all
through school. You see, the Ledbetters' house has a guest
house separate in the back, and they let Bob have it to himself since he got into high school. It's got its own kitchen
and bath, like a separate house."

"You own a car?" asked Feinman.

"Sure—a VW. You aren't asking me for an *alibi?*" said Blackwell incredulously.

"That's just what."

"Well, for God's sake, Bob'll tell you! I got fed up trying to concentrate at home, I told Mom where I was going—I guess later when the Stranges called she'd forgotten—and went over there about nine o'clock."

"Suppose we hear what he has to say. Did you say he's enrolled here too?" said Sue.

"He's in the class you stopped me going to," said Blackwell. "This is—I don't know what. Pauline! It's bad enough she should be dead—I don't understand how that could happen—but your thinking I had anything to do—oh, hell. Hell. There's just nothing to say." He stood looking out the window, saying nothing, while Feinman went to get Ledbetter. When they came in he swung around and said unsmilingly, "These stupid cops think I had something to do with getting Pauline—killed —like she was, Bob. Don't tell me it's crazy."

"Suppose you let us ask the questions," said Feinman.

"What?" said Ledbetter. He looked blankly at them. He looked more the athletic type than intellectual, burly-shouldered and mousy-haired, with a round face slightly more immature than Blackwell's. Like Blackwell, he was casually clad in jeans and sports shirt. "Cops? That's just terrible about Pauline, but what could they think you—"

"Thursday night," said Sue incisively. "Just tell us about Thursday night. Did Bill come to your place?"

Ledbetter said slowly, "That's right. About nine or a little later, I guess. We both had this exam, it was a tough one, this Latin throws me. We studied awhile and then we wanted some hamburgers, Bill went out and got them. I don't know what time—yeah, I do, it was eleven-thirty because we checked to see if the place was still open, and it's open till midnight."

"What place?"

"Corner of Franklin and Western. He came back with the hamburgers—"

"How long after that?"

Ledbetter blinked. "I don't know, I didn't look, I was studying. What is this, anyway?" He was slowly getting mad.

"Damn it, it was only half an hour," said Blackwell. "I had

to wait a few minutes, but it wasn't much after midnight when I got back—"

"I guess so," said Ledbetter, "but I didn't look at the clock. I'm sorry, Bill, but I didn't."

"I wouldn't have had time, even if I'd—and I had the hamburgers—oh, this is senseless," said Blackwell. "To think I'd hurt Pauline—"

"Your car in the lot?" asked Feinman.

"Yes, sure. What now?"

"We'd like to look at it, is all."

"It's unlocked—look where you like."

"What's your address, Mr. Ledbetter?" asked Sue.

"Mine? Well, it's Emmet Terrace—four-three-two."

"Did you know where Pauline was going on Thursday night?" Sue asked Blackwell.

"Yes," he said. "Yes, I did. Out with Sylvia."

"And she was supposed to be in by twelve on week nights. Did you know her parents were out that night too?"

"What? I don't remember," said Blackwell. "Cops! As if it wasn't enough, hearing about it—I nearly stayed home—I wish I had. I wish—oh, hell." He was staring out the window again.

"We'll probably want to talk to you again," said Feinman. In the corridor he added, "What's with the address?"

"It fits," said Sue tersely. "I thought you knew this town, Joe. It's roughly the same neighborhood. The Stranges live on Sycamore Avenue, and Emmet Terrace is six or eight blocks away, those old winding streets up above the boulevard. He admitted they'd had arguments lately. He could have decided to run over to see her, when he went out for the hamburgers. And as it happened she was home alone—it'd have been just after the Nicholses dropped her. And they got into another argument. Spur of the moment deal. He's big and strong—he could have killed her before he realized."

"Yeah," said Feinman, "very easy, I can see that—how often has it happened? But it's a long way from making a legal case. Unless he decides to tell us about it after we lean on him some more."

"Which they sometimes do," said Sue with a sigh. "It's not the only possible answer, but it looks the most probable to me. Do we get a search warrant for his car?"

"We're supposed to do things the legal way. She'd have ridden in it a thousand times, so any evidence like that wouldn't say a damned thing. But just in case, we'd better look," said Feinman.

They went back to the station and applied for the warrant.

About nine-thirty, after Sue and Feinman had taken off for L.A.C.C., Maddox had a call from Dr. Collins.

"I understand you're the officer—er—concerned in the matter. Mrs. Foster asked me to call you. Mrs. Vickers is able to talk to you now, and I must say I'd like to talk to you too. I'm at the hospital now, if you'd—"

"We're hunting some answers, too. I'll be with you in ten minutes. Chapter Two in the saga of Aunt Helen, César. Come on."

They found Dr. Alonzo Collins in the patients' lounge at the end of one wing of the hospital. He was a nondescript elderly man, carelessly if conventionally dressed, but he looked eminently reliable, sane, and kind. FAMILY DOCTOR might have been emblazoned on his bald brow.

He shook hands formally and said, "I didn't know one thing about this—and I'd like to know more. Convalescent homes—well, they're good and bad, but we have a very strict system of inspection. From what I can make out, the one Mrs. Vickers ended up in ought to be put out of business. I was horrified, what she's told me."

"The Board of Health is on it, Doctor."

"Ah—good." He looked relieved. "This all came as a complete surprise to me, you know, I didn't know about her accident. She—"

"You weren't notified? I wondered about that. As her regular doctor—"

"I was out of town until last Friday—first vacation in three years. Mrs. Foster had wired me, but when I got back and saw that, all I could write her was that I didn't know anything about it. But of course there was no reason I should. I'm not affiliated with the General. When she fell, I gather this neighbor naturally called an ambulance, and she was brought here first and then to the General. That's the standard procedure in a good many such cases, where more than a brief hospital visit, and surgery, is indicated. For patients on Medicare, Medicaid. The General's much larger, has more facilities. And of course it was a question of surgery. I'm a G.P. There wasn't any real reason the surgeon or the hospital would have contacted me—in any case I wasn't here. The surgery," he added, "was an excellent job. There's no reason she shouldn't be getting around fine in a few weeks, with some therapy. Who was the surgeon, do you know?"

"A Dr. Brokaw."

"Oh, yes, I've heard of him by reputation, don't know him personally. Supposed to be a good man. He certainly did a good job on that hip." Collins frowned and jingled coins in his pocket. "But the treatment she had in this other place— wherever—by all she tells me, set back her recovery to some extent. How in the world did she land in such a place?"

"Supposedly a mix-up of names. That happen often in hospitals?"

"Good heavens, no," said Collins, astonished. "And how such a place came to be in business at all— Well, you'll want some facts. I'm very glad to know the place is being investigated. I saw Mrs. Vickers first about five yesterday afternoon. Dr. Hirschner, in Emergency here, told me he'd diagnosed an O.D. of morphine and pumped her stomach. As a matter of fact, it was a very slight O.D.—"

"Potentially fatal?"

Collins hesitated. "I wouldn't like to say—so many factors enter in. At her age, and with the treatment we can guess she had in the previous week or so—but her heart's very sound, of course. No, I don't think so. She was extremely dehydrated and the stomach nearly empty. I started her on I.V.'s and plenty of fluids, and she's snapped out of it very well. I'd expect a routine convalescence. But I'd certainly be interested in knowing more about this so-called rest home," said Collins.

"Oh, so will we. Can we see her?"

He nodded. "Room four-twenty down the hall. She was putting away a harvest hand's breakfast half an hour ago."

Room four-twenty had two beds in it, but the one nearest the door had its curtains pulled and the bed held a motionless, sleeping form. In the bed by the window Aunt Helen was sitting propped up against the pillows talking to Myra Foster.

"These are the policemen, Aunt Helen. I don't know what we'd have done without them. Sergeant Maddox and—it was another one—" Myra looked inquiringly at Rodriguez.

"Detective Rodriguez."

"Or what I'd have done. How do you do," said Aunt Helen. "Heavens, I look a sight—my hair not set in all this time, and I was so starved I never thought about putting on any make-up—"

"The hairdresser's coming this afternoon."

"Would either of you happen to have a cigarette? Myra forgot to bring me any."

"Well, I didn't know whether I'd find you dead! The way you looked yesterday—"

Maddox gave her a cigarette and lit it for her, found a saucer to use as an ashtray. She was looking at him and Rodriguez brightly, curiously. Awake, even with the plastered-down hair and no make-up, she was an attractive old lady, her blue eyes bright and aware. "Do you feel like telling us the story?" he asked sympathetically.

"There's not much to tell, really," she said. "And I can't tell you what I suppose you'd really like to know, how I got to that place. Because everybody at the hospital was nice and kind. The doctor was quite nice too, of course I only saw him once before the operation. He was a stranger to me, I'd have liked Dr. Collins there too, but I know that's the way hospitals are now, specialists for everything—and of course it was all so sudden, being an accident. My, this cigarette tastes good—they say you lose the taste after a while, but I don't believe it. They couldn't have been nicer, if it was all pretty impersonal—and even if I wasn't, well, paying. It was the first time I'd had to use this Medicare. The nurse—at the General, I mean—told me I'd probably be in a rest home a few weeks and then I could go home."

"You're coming home with Leo and me," said Myra firmly. "You can sell the house for ten times what Uncle John paid for it."

"Well, I'm thinking about it. One does get into a rut, and with so few old friends left here—maybe a change'd do me good. As long as I can take Sammy."

"Of course you can bring Sammy, I like a cat about the place."

"Poor Sammy!" Aunt Helen smiled. "It was all his fault, but of course he didn't mean it. Well, I was really rather looking forward to the rest home, and the therapy. You know, that one Alida James was in after her stroke was a very nice place, so clean and cheerful. That last morning, it was a Thursday, the nurse got me all ready to go—it had really been very awkward, you see, because there hadn't been anyone to bring my things from home. I didn't like to call and ask Mrs. Wilde, I don't know the woman very well, it was bad enough having to give her my extra key so she could use the phone to call Myra—"

"I told you we've got it back."

"And all I'd taken with me in the ambulance was my bag, I'd had the presence of mind to do that. My checkbook was in it—as well as everything else they had to have," she said rather grimly, "Social Security number, Medicare card, Medicaid card—the red tape—and, nice as they were, you can be sure they took all that down before they put me to bed and had a look at my leg! That one nurse, the young black one, was very obliging—she told me the price and I wrote a check, for a couple of new nightgowns and a housecoat at the gift shop. But that was all I had—not even a comb, let alone a toothbrush. Everything supplied there, but it was awkward. But I thought, all these convalescent places, there are people coming in—church groups, volunteers, social workers—and I was *so hoping* you'd come right out, Myra, but if you didn't I thought I could ask one of those women to go to the house and bring me some clothes. I never realized before just how alone I was." She sighed. "Well, the ambulance came—"

"Did you notice the name on it?" asked Rodriguez. "Mayfair, L.A. County, whatever? And were you the only one in it?"

"No, I didn't notice. The doors were open and the orderlies just lifted me in on a stretcher. And yes, there was another woman—I never got a close look at her, and I felt so sorry for the poor thing, she was crying all the while. I tried to talk to her but she wouldn't answer. Well, when the ambulance drove up to that—that *place* and I got a look at it when they took me out—well, I couldn't believe it. A convalescent home? It looked like—like the old Addams Family cartoons! I don't think that house has had a decent cleaning in fifty years. And as for the people—Mrs. Parks—and all the rest—" She shut her eyes. "A lot of those patients are senile, I suppose—poor old people—but that's no excuse for the kind of treatment they got. I don't suppose I need to go into details, about the— well, the inexcusable lack of attention. There I was helpless, or nearly—I knew I'd need a lot of practice before I could walk on my own again, and I was terrified that if I tried it alone that pin would come out or something. They just dumped me in a bed and left me—and the sheets weren't even clean! The only two nurses who ever tended me—nurse's aides I suppose they'd be, and precious little aid about it— could hardly speak English, one of them Mexican and the other one German or something—and there wasn't even any bell to push, and when I was reduced to calling for help—you haven't any idea how undignified that makes one feel—I could shout myself hoarse before anybody came. Then, like as not, it'd be one of the men—two big young louts—and I must say I never thought I'd live to see the day I had a man lift me onto a bedpan! Not that they bothered half the time. There were a couple of days when nobody came near me at all, ex- cept with the slops they called food—it was like a nightmare —they'd put diapers on me as if I were a baby! The food—I could hardly bring myself to eat it, mostly watery oatmeal and something meant for stew—but I kept telling myself I had to keep my strength up, somehow I'd get out of there and report them all to the authorities. I couldn't make out how the place stayed in business, I know they have to pass inspections! And I knew you wouldn't let me down, Myra. You knew what had happened—that black nurse said she'd mailed my post card. So I knew you'd come as soon as you could, and find me somehow."

"Was there any active cruelty to the patients, or just this general lack of care?" asked Rodriguez. "Did you see much of the other patients?"

"Those poor dreadful old people—" She shuddered. "If I ever start to go senile, Myra, you can feed me strychnine. Once or twice they carried me out to that big room with a lot of them, while the bed was changed. The only times it was changed. Oh, it was more than just carelessness, Mr. Rodriguez. The first time I complained about the food, and there not being a bell, that Mrs. Parks came in and slapped me. She told me to keep quiet and be grateful I was being looked after. She'd hit the others too, if they made too much noise. And the second time they took me out there, this old man kept moaning and yelling he wanted to go home, and I saw Mrs. Parks give him a hypodermic shot—I don't know what it was, but it put him to sleep."

"You don't say," said Maddox. "You're a tough lady, Mrs. Vickers. I'd have been gibbering mad by then."

"Eleven days," she said rather proudly. "I counted them. If it hadn't been that I knew Myra and Leo'd be coming, I daresay I should have been. You've no idea how helpless I felt —trapped there, as it were. Oh, I didn't tell you that. The day I got there, Mrs. Parks took off the little bracelet they'd put on at the hospital, with my name on it, you know, and put on another. It wasn't until about an hour later I happened to look at it, and it said RUTH RUNNELS on it. Not my name at all. So the next time she came by I complained about that, and she just said not to be silly and went away. And after that she always called me Miss Runnels—it sounds like a little thing, but it was rather the last straw—a couple of times I just screamed at her, I'm Helen Vickers, but she didn't pay any attention. I was so furious—if I could have got *at her*—!"

Maddox and Rodriguez exchanged a blank look, and Rodriguez shrugged. "What happened yesterday?" asked Maddox.

"You tell me!" said Aunt Helen. "I remember waking up, and that's about all. I was starving to death—the last two days they'd brought me sauerkraut, which I won't eat under any conditions, and oatmeal that was half water. By then I knew if I wanted any attention I had to keep yelling, as if I really meant it, for half an hour before anyone'd come. But nobody did until that German girl and Mrs. Parks came in all in a hurry—the girl was scared for some reason—and Mrs. Parks grabbed my arm and stuck a needle in it. And that's all I know, until I came to right here, with Myra crying all over me like a silly fool."

"Well, I thought you were dying," said Myra. Her eyes flashed on Maddox and Rodriguez. "Have they shut that place up yet? All those people ought to be in jail! And how on earth anybody ever got sent there—who makes these arrangements, the doctor, the hospital? They ought to know where they're sending people—"

"You'd certainly think so," said Maddox. "We'll be asking some questions. But I'm glad you're going to be all right, Mrs. Vickers."

"Oh, you couldn't kill me with an ax," she said cheerfully. "I'm just glad I seem to have been the catalyst, if that's the word I want, to get that place looked into. May I have another cigarette, please?"

They heard her laughing as they went out. "And just who did send her there?" said Rodriguez. "Or anybody? This just makes it look more shapeless, Ivor."

"Doesn't it? Implication is, when the Fosters broke in demanding Aunt Helen, they all got nervous and bundled her off—to the other place? What's the connection? And denied she'd ever been there when we came into the picture."

"They got the address from the doctor's office."

"So they did. Let's," said Maddox, "go talk to the doctor."

The daily grind of the routine was always with them, the endless reports to write. At least it had stopped raining; it was bright and clear and very cold. Sergeant Ellis was in court downtown at the arraignment of the narco peddler they'd dropped on last month. It was D'Arcy's day off. The warrant on Slaney had come through and been dully dispatched to the D.A.'s office. Slaney would probably be indicted Thursday or Friday, but the D.A.'s office would have to pass the charge on the warrant or amend it. Daisy had been hurriedly summoned downtown again when it looked as if that trial might get under way after all. Rowan was down at headquarters arranging a line-up to get Dolores Mulvaney's identification of the Williams couple.

Feinman and Sue had applied for a search warrant of Blackwell's car, and now Sue wanted to talk to some of Pauline's girl friends, with more definite questions in mind. She snatched a sandwich at a drugstore and went up to Hollywood High to see Pauline's closest friend, Alice Goodman; but Alice wasn't in school. She saw the girls' vice-principal.

"Alice's mother called—Alice is terribly broken up about Pauline. Such a dreadful thing—Mr. Strange called to inform me this morning. A nice quiet girl too, we never had any trouble with her, not like some of these girls."

She went back to the station, found the number, and called the Goodman house. There was also, she reflected, that pair on the double date last Wednesday—a Jim Warden and his girl; she ought to see them.

"Oh, dear, I don't think Alice could talk to you now," said Mrs. Goodman distractedly. "She hasn't stopped crying since we heard about it. I couldn't believe it—Pauline, murdered! Such a nice family, and strict with her, not as if she'd been the kind to go racketing around with a wild crowd—"

"When do you think I can talk to her?"

"Oh, dear, I don't know. Alice wouldn't know anything about it, anyway."

"Well, Pauline may have told her something—about a new friend, or any plans she had for that night," said Sue vaguely.

"Oh. Well, I expect you could see her tonight, I hope she'll be feeling better by then."

"Eight o'clock? Fine, thank you. . . . Damn," said Sue, putting down the phone. Tomorrow was her day off, and she had a dozen things to do. She'd meant to save some time by getting the laundry done tonight, and now that had to go by the board. Really, she thought, they ought to start looking for a place to buy before prices went any higher. Family or no family—and of course a lot of what they saw on the job should discourage anybody from trying to bring up children in a decent way these days— Now if they were in a proper-sized house with their own washer and dryer, she could get a couple of loads done tonight, even when she had to go out. As it was, she'd have to take a chance on finding the laundromat reasonably uncrowded tomorrow morning.

Relax and don't worry, said the doctor. Little did he know the job. An interesting job—if sometimes messy and sordid, more interesting than working in an office somewhere, and she liked it. But suddenly she thought—quite aside from the fact that they really did want a family—it would be a nice excuse to get away from the job for a while. She could go on working the first three months, but after that—a leave of absence up to a year, and then if she wanted to come back— Well, it was a thought.

Just then Feinman came in to say that the warrant had come through, so they got Dabney and the mobile lab truck and went back to L.A.C.C.

Patrolman Gonzales was cruising down Hollywood Boulevard in the far right lane, idly watching traffic and glad that it had stopped raining, about one o'clock. He was just thinking of calling in a code seven and stopping for a hamburger. He caught the light at Fairfax and had his hand on the mike when a horn honked violently close beside him. He jumped and looked around.

Pulled up beside him in the lane to his left was a little Honda, and the pretty redhead was leaning over from behind the wheel. "I found it!" she called triumphantly. "In the last spoonful of gunk, I found it!"

Gonzales grinned at her and raised a circled thumb and forefinger as the light changed.

The doctor's office was on Wilshire, nearly out to Westwood. It was high up in a new brick and glass office building, and the door bore severely handsome lower-case lettering: Dr. Colby Brokaw. But the room beyond was only nine feet by seven, if thickly carpeted, holding one small couch and chair, a table minus an ashtray. These offices would rent for a fortune.

There was another door at the back with a pane of frosted amber glass, a bell push in the wall beside it. Maddox pushed that and the amber panel slid back efficiently. "Yes?" The white-uniformed, capped woman beamed at them, friendly. Maddox showed her the badge and the beam vanished. "Oh, yes? What was it you wanted?"

"To see the doctor." Maddox regarded her with some interest. She was a mountainously fat woman, difficult to guess her age past all the blubber, but she had young-looking skin, and might have been pretty without the three chins; her hair was glossy black. "This is about his patient Mrs. Vickers," he added. "Was it you who gave the address of the convalescent home to the Fosters yesterday?" Somehow he felt that, even in her agitation, Myra would have mentioned this one.

"Why, no, it couldn't have been," she said, looking surprised. "I'm afraid I don't know— The doctor doesn't have office hours on Monday, I wasn't here. I believe the accountant was here, Mrs. Stapleton, but she doesn't normally have anything to do with the patients' files. I don't know if the doctor can see you."

"Suppose you go and ask," suggested Maddox.

"Well—his next appointment isn't for forty-five minutes," she said dubiously. "Just a moment."

While they waited Rodriguez lit a cigarette and looked in vain for an ashtray. "Doctors," said Maddox. "They believe their own propaganda, César." Resignedly Rodriguez went out to the hall and found a tub of sand. They waited.

"I wonder," said Rodriguez, "what D'Arcy's doing on his day off. You know, Ivor, it's very funny about D'Arcy."

"What in particular?"

"Well, I've never known him to go on this long without all of a sudden falling for some damn-fool unsuitable female— usually blond."

"True," said Maddox. "Maybe age is curing him. I'll tell you one thing. I think he deliberately picked a fight with that last one he had on the string, the Fitzpatrick girl. Because she'd found out what his name is and insisted on using it."

Rodriguez laughed. D'Arcy was sensitive about his peculiar first name and had them all trained never to mention it. "You could be right. But he's overdue for falling in love again—I wonder what he'll pick this time."

The nurse slid back the panel. "You may come in." She opened the door and they passed through to a narrow hall. "The first door on the left."

That opened into a small but well-furnished office, with a walnut desk, three matching padded chairs, one puzzling Chagall on the inner wall, and a wide window overlooking the city. From this high up, the city looked clean and serene on this clear day. The handsomest item in the room was Dr. Brokaw. He was tall and thin, with graying black hair, a small neat mustache, and a nobly arched nose. He was beautifully tailored in light gray.

"Sergeant Maddox—Detective Rodriguez," said Maddox.

"Sit down, won't you? I'm afraid," said Brokaw, "I don't know what this is all about, but any way I can help you— What *is* it all about?" He sat behind the desk.

"One of your patients. Mrs. Helen Vickers."

There was no recognition in his eyes; he looked apologetic. "I'd have to look up my records. You see, I'm not in ordinary private practice, except for a few patients. If Mrs. Vickers was at the General hospital, one of the others I'm affiliated with— well, I often see thirty or forty patients a day, and on surgery days I may do from three to seven operations." He went to the door and spoke to the nurse. "I know," he said, reseating himself and looking even more apologetic, "it all sounds impersonal, but that's the way it is. One gets to seeing them as— well, bodies in need of attention."

"It was the General hospital. She had a broken hip. An old lady sixty-six, otherwise quite healthy," said Maddox.

"Oh. There have been several of that general—but I do seem to recall that one. Yes indeed. She came through surgery quite well, I'd have expected a very good prognosis. But may I ask what the police—it was just a routine case—" He looked from Maddox to Rodriguez, and now he was interested.

"Well, you—or somebody—arranged for her to be sent to a convalescent home."

He nodded. "Quite likely. Also routine. The hospitals always need the beds. When a patient no longer needs the actual hospital care, they're better off at a good rest home and it's not as expensive."

"The one Mrs. Vickers wound up in," said Maddox, "might be called damned expensive. It's about to be shut down by the Board of Health, and there'll probably be a charge laid of mistreating patients."

"What?" Brokaw looked outraged and astonished. "But these places are all regularly inspected—some of them better than others, but they all have to conform to certain standards. Good God, I'm very sorry to hear that—but also very surprised. What put you onto it?"

"A couple of determined relatives. The interesting thing is," said Rodriguez, with an amiable smile, "they got the address of the place from your records." The nurse waddled in with a slim manila folder and laid it on the desk, vanished discreetly. "Yesterday morning. Your nurse apparently wasn't here, but somebody else was, and got badgered into looking up the record."

"My records?" Brokaw stared, opened the folder. "Well, yes, here it is, I see. Helen Vickers, fracture right—and so on and so on— But I've never heard of this place," said Brokaw.

"You didn't arrange her transfer to the home?"

"Good heavens, no, that kind of thing's hardly my responsibility. Usually the individual home is selected by the patient, or the relatives. The hospital doesn't recommend any particular ones. They're chosen for location, or price, or some such reason. The only reason the address happens to be here in my files was to complete the record—it would have been added automatically at the hospital when she was transferred."

"I see. You're not familiar with the place personally."

"Obviously not, if it's what you describe. It's not necessary for me to follow up these cases, all good convalescent homes have their own therapists and consulting physicians. But that is really appalling," said Brokaw, "that such a place should have been in operation—I can't understand it. Er—is Mrs. Vickers—?"

"Seems to be quite all right now."

"Appalling. You said, the patients mistreated—an elderly woman like that, enough to cause some deterioration. We like to think these things can't happen anymore," said Brokaw with a grimace. "But I'm afraid I couldn't help you any more than I have."

"Well, thanks very much." Maddox stood up.

❖❖❖

"I do not like thee, Dr. Fell," said Rodriguez. "But I don't know why."

"Neither do I," said Maddox. "It's all very plausible. Busy man. Good surgeon."

"Now why in hell," said Rodriguez, "kidnap Aunt Helen? She hasn't got any money. But her I like." He chuckled. "A very spunky old girl."

"Yes," said Maddox, and was silent all the way up through Hollywood.

"Are you lost in Holmesian deduction?" asked Rodriguez. "That was Cahuenga we just passed. You've overshot home base."

"I know," said Maddox. "I just thought I'd swing by La Mirada. It occurred to me suddenly—I'd been aiming at one little idea, sicking the newscaster onto it, but there could have been another result. People being people."

"I suppose you know what you're talking about."

Maddox turned down the block on La Mirada where Anton Czerny's house sat on the corner. He pulled the Maserati into the curb.

There was a neat small trailer parked in the driveway in front of the little garage, and men were up on the telephone pole attaching wires. The front door of the house was open, and there seemed to be people in there. Two men and a woman came down the steps carrying pails and brooms.

They got out of the car.

Doug Wyler came out on the porch. He was filthy in old jeans and a torn T-shirt. "Hey, the cops," he said, and came down to them. "Did you ever see anything like it? Look at it! Isn't it beautiful?"

"What's going on?" asked Rodriguez.

"After that TV show, everything just got organized," said Wyler. "Well, I didn't need the show—I was going to take a week off, help the old man. But everybody else around here, I guess you could say they got motivated. We got twenty, thirty people out, from all around the neighborhood, to help clean up the place. And there's this auto agency donated a trailer for him to live in till the house is fixed up—installation for free, they're just getting it all hooked up now, sewer and all. I helped him about the insurance, the papers were gone but he remembered the company, and they've been just great—wonderful. Sent a man right out, and he'd seen the broadcast too, he says they'll be right on it, a crew out this week to repair the ceilings and walls and all."

"Well, I will be damned," said Maddox. "I will be—all I was thinking about was parents' consciences. I must have forgotten there'd be some others around."

"Come again?" said Rodriguez.

"Parents. Maybe some left with a modicum of morality and responsibility, so when they heard the famous newscaster say the police believed juveniles from a local school were the culprits—and I emphasized that to him—they might get to questioning their offspring and eventually, just maybe, give us somewhere to look. That was all that was in my mind. Afterward, I thought—but I didn't expect anything like this." There hadn't, of course, been much the police could do about this: they'd taken photographs, Dabney and Rowan had poked around, but it had been anonymous filth and destruction.

Anton Czerny came out of the trailer. He was wearing a rather dazed smile. "They have the telephone fixed," he said to Wyler.

"Oh, fine," said Wyler, and started back to the house.

"It is very hard to understand," said Czerny. He probably didn't recognize them as the police who came the other day. "These people—tell me to call them Doug and Linda—they only live near me maybe a year and a half. Just young people, why do they care about an old man? Come to help. Good people—a lot of others—all come to help." His eyes were filled with tears.

"Always more good people than bastards," said Maddox, feeling slightly awed.

CHAPTER 6

When they came into the precinct house, Sergeant Whitwell,
on the desk, hailed Maddox. "Call for you just ten minutes
ago, somebody at the Board of Health. You're supposed to call
back."

"O.K." Maddox took the number; they climbed stairs. Nobody else was in. Two manila-foldered reports lay on Maddox'
desk; he picked them up. The first was the autopsy report on
Margaret Peller. A slightly more complicated autopsy than
usual, and sentimental Dr. Bergner felt rather strongly about
battered children; he'd given priority to Peggy. Maddox read
the report rapidly. What it translated to was that she'd been
knocked around, beaten up, probably with fists, hit her head
on something, and died of a fractured skull. Probable time of
death, noon to 8 P.M. last Thursday, just as expected. The
other report was from the lab, also on Peller; it didn't say
much except that they had evaluated some more prints, lifted
from the metal clasp of her handbag. Good prints, but unfortunately they didn't seem to be in anybody's records. "Useful,"
said Maddox, passing both over to Rodriguez. They knew now
she couldn't have had much cash there; the bits and pieces of
inexpensive jewelry had been added to the pawnbrokers' hot
list but it wasn't likely that would turn up X.

He dialed the number Whitwell had given him and was
presently connected to Mr. Rodney Peasmarsh, who had a
precise schoolmaster's voice and evidently didn't believe in
wasting time. "This Sunnyvale rest home, Sergeant. In our
view, it's not merely a question of condemnation and closure.
I feel there's room for felony charges, and we'd like to know if
you've got anything to add on that."

"Probably, yes. There's a good witness to active mistreat-

ment of the patients, on the part of the Parks woman at least.
You've already been into it, then."

"Oh, yes, of course. Good. Some more may turn up. I have
just been in contact with the district attorney's office, we don't
like to fiddle around wasting time on these things. I'd appreciate it if you could join me for a conference tomorrow at nine,
in Mr. Ravenna's office—the deputy district attorney. With
whatever you've got."

"That's all right with me."

"Good. I'll see you then." Peasmarsh rang off firmly. Maddox sat back and massaged his jaw. It was getting on toward
the end of shift again, what with all the driving around they'd
done. Sue came plodding up the stairs and looked in.

"You should have a memo from R. and I. downtown somewhere here."

"What on? You," said Maddox, "look beat, my love."

"Beat!" said Sue. "What a day!"

❖❖❖

There hadn't been anything very revealing at first glance in
Blackwell's VW, and they left Dabney vacuuming the interior
and came back to the office. Five minutes later the Alameda
jail called. The woman booked as Elizabeth Williams had decided she wanted to do some talking, and was asking
specifically for the policewoman she'd talked to up in Hollywood.

So Sue drove downtown, with some difficulty found a slot in
the big parking lot, and announced herself at the jail. The
Williams girl was brought to her in one of the cell-like interro-
gation rooms, and said in her flat nasal voice, "You was nice,
before. Polite to me. I'm through with that dude, and I figured
if I blew the whistle on him you might forget to charge me
with anything. I didn't do nothing to that girl anyway."

"We don't make deals, Mrs. Williams, but we'd like any information you can give us."

"Listen, don't call me that, I'm not Mrs. anybody, and anyway he's not Williams. He's Billy Lee Hodgkins. They want
him for a lot of stuff all over. My name's Millie Bronson. I
took up with him about six months ago, I got stranded in a
one-horse town in Illinois, singing with a combo only we

couldn't get any steady spots. He—Billy Lee—he talks a great fight, all the big contacts he's got on the Coast, get me a great job, maybe make TV, and I had to fall for it. He's a smooth talker when he wants. All it's been since is picking up johns for eating money, and him cutting the take sixty–forty." She sat hunched over on the straight chair, in the plain beige jail uniform. "I don't figure I owe him anything."

"How old are you, Millie?"

"Twenty next month, why?"

Automatically Sue thought, forcing a minor into prostitution; but Millie was probably older in experience than Sue would be when she died of old age. "You want to tell me about this rape."

"Sure. I'd been good and fed up and said so. He'd slapped me around, too, but I was scared to walk out on him. He can be mean, 'specially in liquor. We'd had a fight that day, and he said he could pick up something better than me anytime he wanted, he went out and came back with that girl. I was kind of sorry for her—but I was scared of him, he got to putting down the straight Bourbon. Then she brought the fuzz down, and now I think about it, it's my chance to get loose from him. I know he's wanted in Texas, he said so. You tell them his right name and ask."

Sue watched the matron take her out, and proceeded down to R. and I. to see what had showed on Williams. Old in experience as she was, Millie didn't know much about routine police procedure; the computers took the place of word of mouth these days.

The pretty flaxen-haired policewoman heard what she had to say and pulled the file. "You should have had a follow-up on it, but I will say we're backlogged some here, it might not have gone through until this afternoon." Williams had been printed when he was booked, of course, and the prints automatically transmitted to the National Crime Information Center. The identification had come back right away: he had a pedigree a yard long and about twenty known aliases. He was wanted in Dallas for Murder One, in Memphis for rape and bunko, in Massachusetts for rape and manslaughter, in New York for pimping and aggravated assault. So it didn't look as if L.A. would be holding him to prosecute for raping Dolores; Texas had priority.

She told Maddox about that, kicking off her shoes and rolling a report form into the typewriter. "And now I've got to go out again tonight."

"Leave it. Somebody else can follow up Pauline tomorrow."

"We're all busy enough, and lord knows what might go down tonight. I said I'd go to see the Goodman girl."

Not that she expected much from her, but it was another place to ask questions. When they went home she got steaks out of the freezer, the easiest thing; and she sometimes thought (though she wouldn't risk spoiling him by saying so) that her mother was right, saying she'd married a paragon. Ivor, bless him, said he'd see to the dishes.

The Goodman girl was still sniffling and being fussed over by an anxious mother; an excuse to call attention to herself, Sue decided: not as pretty a girl as Pauline, a little too fat. And she didn't know anything. "The last time I saw her was Th-Thursday"—she hiccuped—"and she was just like always —she told me about her date the night before, where they went, she s-said she didn't like to double-date, and—and this friend of Bill's was awfully good-looking but kind of smarty, and she didn't like the girl much either—and she said—oh, oh, to think it was the last time I'd ever see her—it was in the cafeteria—"

"What else did she say?" asked Sue patiently.

"Well, just, she said she thought Bill set up the double date because he didn't want her to have the chance to t-talk about getting m-married—she wanted to so much—"

"Were you home on Thursday night?" Yes, Alice was. Complete with parents and two younger sisters. She admitted apologetically that she didn't have a regular boy friend.

Everything they heard about Pauline led right back to Bill Blackwell. One thing police work made abundantly clear was that the simplest, likeliest explanation was usually the right one.

Being out, she might as well kill two birds. She had the address from the L.A.C.C. registrar, and looked up Jim Warden, for his version of the double date. The address was Harold Way, a sleazy old narrow street off Western; it turned out to be a bastard-Spanish four-family place, and the Wardens occupied a top front. Jim Warden was a little surprise to Sue.

"A lady cop," he said, looking at the badge. "Welcome to the pad, if you don't think you need a chaperone." There was a little metal plaque in the middle of the front door: IF YOU DON'T SWING DON'T RING! "My good mama's out on the town with the current boy friend. What can I do for you?"

Not the likeliest new pal for Bill Blackwell—but it was his first college term, and Warden was the life-of-the-party type that was attractive on the surface to most people. He was almost girlishly handsome, with long-lashed brown eyes, a wide mobile mouth, a ready smile, a charming voice: tall and lithe, and unlike Blackwell a natty dresser. Home alone, evidently studying, by the open book on the little desk, he was wearing good sports clothes and jewelry. Men wearing the unisex jewelry now, necklaces, bracelets.

She asked him sedately about last Wednesday night, and he shrugged, smiled, talked easily. "Billy boy not much of a swinger, shall we say, or his little chick either—it was his idea, but a sad mistake. They didn't want to go to a disco, don't like to dance, all pathetic, lady, pathetic. And the dear little dewy-eyed thing had to be home on the stroke of midnight or big bad parents spank." He laughed, showing even, fine white teeth. "After I dropped Billy off at his pad Patty and I made a better night of it—li'l old disco up on the Strip. But just why in all the world's the L.A.P.D. interested in my dates, lady? Not that my life isn't one big open book, but I'm curious." He put his head on one side rather winsomely.

Sue told him, and the smile vanished; he said, "Oh. Oh, I didn't know—that." After a moment he said, "I'm sorry."

"Did she and Bill have any—oh, arguments, that night?"

He shook his head. "Why? Do the police think—he had anything to do with it?"

"We have to ask all sorts of questions, of everybody," said Sue. He wouldn't be a good source of answers; he was eternally too conscious of himself and his looks and his charm to be noticing much about anybody else.

Peasmarsh turned out to be a short, spare, gray man with thin silver hair and silver-rimmed glasses. He was also evidently extremely efficient, and after listening politely to Maddox outline the start of the case he coughed, folded his legs the opposite way, and lifted his pleasant tenor voice in a concise recital of his own activities.

"It was immediately obvious, of course, that the place could not begin to comply with our regulation standards. The condition of the building, the state of the patients, the lack of staff, all most deplorable. The patients, of course, were our first concern." The patients had been, though he didn't put it that way, parceled out to the General hospital, other county hospitals, for exact evaluations of condition; eventually they'd be transferred to other convalescent homes. The records, such as they had found, were very incomplete and unsatisfactory; it wasn't at all clear which patient was which. Some were undoubtedly senile and might not know their own names; others could probably be questioned eventually. He placed a little stack of papers on the table: an ordinary dime-store tablet, a cheap address book. The deputy D.A. looked at both and pushed them over to Maddox, who riffled through the tablet. Lists of names scribbled down, page by page, dates; some were crossed out.

"That was all the records of patients?" The deputy D.A. was incredulous. "No medical records, case histories?"

"None. The property was rented by the Parks woman— Rose Ellen Parks. It is owned by an investment corporation. Of course it is potentially valuable property, in business zoning, but at today's inflated prices and the difficulties with building permits, I can surmise they were happy enough to realize something from it." Peasmarsh's tone was dry. "There were only four employees on the premises, and she said that was the entire staff." He passed over the list of names, correctly one for the deputy D.A., one for the police. "We had a little trouble prying addresses out of them, but I was—er—persistent." Fred Klepper, Gerda Klepper, Robert Pine, Anita Arrubes. "A citation will be filed—has been filed—against the place, and the Parks woman informed of that, but the main reason I wanted this meeting was to find out if the police have any fuller information that might lead to further charges. I do feel strongly that there may be a case against Mrs. Parks for another charge."

"Yes indeedy," said Maddox. "We have one witness who can

testify that the Parks woman offered violence to the patients. Is she a registered nurse?"

"Unfortunately yes," said Peasmarsh. "It's quite incomprehensible that a woman trained in the profession should so far forget all humanity—"

"You just haven't seen enough of human nature," said Maddox. "Then we probably couldn't charge her with dispensing medication illegally—those hypos. But there's no indication that a doctor ever visited the place, saw the patients. And it's going to be interesting to hear what some of the patients can tell us. Have you had any opinion from the hospitals about them?"

Peasmarsh shook his head. "It's too early. They were only transferred to other institutions yesterday."

"Will the police follow that up, Sergeant?" said the deputy D.A. Maddox nodded; they'd be asking for some help on that from headquarters. He slid the tablet, the address book, into his breast pocket; Peasmarsh made no objection.

"Now my further concern is the implied connection between this place and the other convalescent home. I don't quite understand the nature of it, Sergeant—"

"And it interests us," said Maddox. "And neither do we."

"But the point is, is there any connection at all? I have been back in our files, and this Sunnyvale Convalescent Home—er, the one on Hillhurst Avenue—has an excellent record with us. But naturally, if there is any connection, financial or otherwise, it follows that we'll make a much closer inspection of that place as well."

"You wouldn't find anything out of line," said Maddox, "but we'll be following that up too, Mr. Peasmarsh."

"You'll both be in touch, then," said the deputy D.A. "It looks to me as if we've got a good case for an aggravated assault charge on the Parks woman and possibly some of the staff. Yes, depending on what we hear from the other witnesses, of course. Well, as soon as you've got anything more, Sergeant—keep us notified."

Maddox went back to Wilcox Street and collected Rodriguez, who had been out on a felony drunk driving and just sent a body to the morgue. "You," he complained, "came back too soon. I think something's just going to break up there."

Maddox brought him up to date on the strange case of Aunt

Helen. "We are now," he said, "about to hear Mrs. Cleveland's version. I think it might be interesting."

For a few minutes, at the smartly hygienic convalescent home on Hillhurst, it seemed they wouldn't be hearing anything; the blond receptionist told them that Mrs. Cleveland was extremely busy and couldn't be disturbed. "We won't go away, you know," said Maddox. "You just tell her we're here."

Grudgingly she used the intercom, and two minutes later Mrs. Cleveland swept out commandingly. "Yes?" She was graciously inquiring. "What can I do for you?"

"You knew we'd be back," said Maddox. "This may be a long session, can we all sit down somewhere?"

She unbent with a slight smile. "I do realize that the police —like hospitals—must have a great deal of red tape. Won't you come into my office?"

It was a cool, pleasant little room, a bright carpet, a small blond desk, a seascape on one wall, openwork drapes. "Now," she said with a graceful gesture, sitting at the desk. "What more information do you need? I will say, it's quite obvious that the initial error was made at the General hospital. It was most unfortunate, and of course embarrassing for us."

"Oh, it was?" said Maddox. "How do you make that out?"

"Why, it was simply a confusion of the I.D. bracelets. We knew her as Ruth Runnels. It was only when Mr. and Mrs. Foster discovered that this other patient, at the other home, was not Mrs. Vickers, that—"

Maddox sat back, regarding her interestedly. "You're saying that Mrs. Vickers—under the wrong name—was here all along."

"Yes, of course. I told you that on Monday," she said slightly surprised. "I can show you the records—of course the medical case history actually belonged to this Runnels woman, and I should like to correct that for our files, but our records, the day-to-day records on Mrs. Vickers, are all in order. I've been talking to the General about their records on her. The Runnels woman—"

"Don't tell me she had a broken right hip too?" asked Rodriguez sardonically. "So you didn't notice any discrepancy, as it were?"

"As a matter of fact, yes," said Mrs. Cleveland evenly. "It's not all that uncommon an injury in old ladies, Mr. Rodriguez. Naturally we didn't have any suspicion, until—"

"But Mrs. Vickers," said Maddox, "says quite definitely she was at the other convalescent home. She never was here at all until last Monday morning, and she doesn't remember that."

"Really, Sergeant"—she raised her brows at him icily—"it can be quite easily substantiated. I'm head nurse here, and there are eight other R.N.'s on duty, at least three on each shift, which is required by law as I'm sure you know. There are also twenty-four nurse's aides and orderlies. I don't say that every single one of those people can swear to the woman's presence, but certainly a good many of them can, and most certainly the three R.N.'s and seven or eight of the aides who were looking after her. And I can, of course."

Rodriguez made an incredulous sound. "I don't know what she may have told her relatives," Mrs. Cleveland went on, "or the police, Sergeant, but I should have thought that the police at least would take into account the—well, the source of information."

"Are you claiming that Mrs. Vickers couldn't be sure where she was?"

She gave them a sudden warm smile. "Now look, Sergeant. I've had a good deal more experience with ill people, and old people, than you can possibly have. That's my job. I can show you the records, and you're quite welcome to talk to the staff —they'll all tell you the same thing. When the woman was brought in she was a good deal confused mentally, and not sure where she was, no. Understandably, from what we know now, she objected to being called Miss Runnels, and was quite obstreperous. We had to sedate her. Oh, that was quite within our rights, the hospital had sent a prescription along with her, for pain. Amytal. She quieted down after a few days and we hadn't any more trouble with her, but she was still mentally disturbed and needed a good deal of attention. For instance, she would refuse her meals and then complain that she wasn't being fed. In the end, one of the girls had to feed her. Then she would claim that one of the girls was mistreating her." She shrugged. "That kind of thing's very typical."

"Really," said Maddox. "It seems a little odd that she has such a clear memory of the other place."

"What other—oh, the other convalescent home. I don't know anything about it," said Mrs. Cleveland. "As I said, the first intimation I had that anything was wrong was when this Mrs. Parks called that morning. She had naturally checked back with the General and discovered that the two patients had been transferred at the same time. When the relatives told her that she had"—she smiled—"the wrong Mrs. Vickers, and the hospital told her that the other patient was here, she called me."

"Naturally," said Maddox. "Strangely enough, the other one is called the Sunnyvale Convalescent Home too."

"Oh?" She looked surprised. "I didn't catch the name Mrs. Parks—I didn't know there was another one."

"There isn't, now. But it was quite different from this place, and Mrs. Vickers gave us a good description of it."

She frowned, looking out the window, and then she said, "May I just suggest something? When we know there was this mistake made—isn't it possible that the ambulance attendants carried her inside, at first, and then took her out to the ambulance again? That could be how she had seen the place."

Maddox sat up and lit a cigarette. "That's a little idea," he said casually. "So she was delivered here on the eighteenth, and she was right here—being tenderly cared for—up until last Monday morning. If confused and not really knowing where she was."

"Yes. It's all in the records. The girls are trained to note down every reaction." She got out a cigarette and he flicked his lighter for her.

"Had you got her started on any therapy?" asked Rodriguez.

"No, we hadn't tried as yet. Her attitude—didn't indicate it."

"Her mind's quite clear now," said Rodriguez.

"I'm glad to hear that. Sometimes with elderly people any shock—a fall, or of course major surgery, which she had—can cause confusion just temporarily. I've seen a good deal of that."

"Do you call sixty-six elderly nowadays? It's mandatory, I think," said Maddox, "that patients in convalescent homes are seen by a doctor at stated intervals. Do you have a regular physician coming in?"

"Several, of course. I can give you their names. We under-

stood that she hadn't had a regular physician, and as Dr.
Phelps had several patients in the same wing, he would have
taken her on. But the once he was here since she came in, he
was in a great hurry and she was asleep, so it was put off."

"Did you mention her name to him?"

"I really don't remember," she said apologetically. "We'd
had a patient die just that afternoon, I'd been with the relatives when he came in." She put out her cigarette.

"We'd like to talk to your staff," said Maddox.

"Certainly. We don't have any regular visiting hours, people
are welcome to come any time. You remember the room she
was in—two-twelve, the cross wing to the left from the
lobby." She was still sitting at her desk, looking cool and
remote, when they went out.

Neither of them made any comment as they walked down
the clean tiled halls to that wing. At the nurses' station there,
two capped white-clad women were talking, a blue-uniformed
woman behind the desk making notes. Maddox introduced
himself, asked questions. The patient who had been removed
last Monday—the one there had been the mistake about, the
wrong name. How long had she been there?

"It'd be in the records, sir," said the plumper nurse. "But it
was nine or ten days as I recall, at least."

"Eleven," said the woman behind the desk. "I remember
when she was checked in, the eighteenth. That was funny,
I've never known such a thing to happen before."

"We'd like to talk to some of the nurse's aides who took care
of her," said Maddox.

"Well, Ada's off on her break, but Jeanie and Heather are
somewhere around—"

In the end they talked to four nurse's aides, three young,
one middle-aged, all looking and sounding like ordinary honest females, if surprised at police asking questions. Yes indeed,
the lady known as Miss Runnels had been here for about ten
days. She'd been some trouble at first, out of her head some of
the time, and having to be fed, but that wasn't anything new
—a lot of old people were like that.

They went out through the flowered lobby and stood on the
shallow steps. Rodriguez was whistling softly through his
teeth. Maddox lit a cigarette.

"I wonder," said Rodriguez, "what effect that would have

on a jury. What am I saying, a jury—on a condemnation case, ordinary assault."

"I wonder," said Maddox, "where's the money, César? What's worth all that?"

"You don't buy it, of course."

"The hell of it is," said Maddox, "I might buy it—until I remember Aunt Helen. It's all very damn plausible. We've only seen Aunt Helen once, and she strikes me as very much the genuine article, very much stable and same. But in there" —he nodded—"are the big guns. All so very plausible."

"And no remote connection between the two homes."

"But even if there is, and it looks impossible there could be— Why? Why all the big guns summoned up to prove Aunt Helen was here?"

"We haven't," said Rodriguez after a moment, "asked any questions at the General."

"At least we know there we'll get some honest answers," said Maddox. "Or do we? And come to think, we haven't had lunch, and it must be three o'clock."

❖❖❖

Just after noon, with D'Arcy and Feinman thinking of going out for lunch, Maddox' original little idea paid off with the arrival of Mr. and Mrs. Stanley Gruber and their thirteen-year-old offspring Freddy.

"We've been after him about this three days," said Gruber savagely. "We saw that telecast Sunday night—my God, what a thing—what a *thing*—and how it said you thought it was kids from Le Conte."

"It was just a joke at first," said his wife. She was a small dark tight-lipped woman in dowdy black and white. She spoke in a choked voice, pressed a handkerchief to her mouth. "To think of having to come to a police station—and tell such a thing about your own boy— It was a joke, I said to Freddy, at least you'd never get up to any such devilment as that, I said—"

"And right away he got this look on his face. I couldn't believe he'd have been on such a—but by God," said Gruber, who was big and ruddy-faced and loud-voiced, "by God if he knew anything about it I was going to get it out of him! It took me three days to do it, and I hope I've scared the living bejesus out of him! Listened to him bawling all night, after the belting I gave him, and this morning he's too sick to go to school, I said sick be damned, if he didn't tell what he knew he'd get another belting, and he finally came apart." He turned fiercely on Freddy, who was small and dark and pale. "So now you tell them! Go on and tell them! Mixed up with a stunt like that, my kid—"

"It wasn't me," said Freddy in a very small voice. "I was just in there once."

"In that house that was all smashed up?" asked Feinman.

"Yessir." It was a whisper. "I just—knew about it. A lot of the kids did. Danny and me—went in there—on a dare. Because we wasn't supposed to."

"How'd you know about it?" asked D'Arcy.

"A lot of kids did. How you got in—at the back door—I was scared but Danny and me went in. Just a minute—so Bob couldn't say we was cowards."

D'Arcy and Feinman looked at each other. "What were you scared of?" asked Feinman.

Freddy burst into tears. "All—all of 'em! And you're not s'posed to snitch on nobody, not right—you make me tell and they'll all *kill* me, beat me up till I'm dead! They would!"

"Like to see anybody kill you with me around," growled Gruber, "not that I'm feeling so damn fond of you right now. You tell the police everything you know right now!"

Freddy sobbed and dragged his palms down his cheeks. "The—the seniors—it was—just some of 'em, I guess—Sam Wells an' Jerry Noonan an' Walt Altshuler 'n' I dunno who else—an' some girls—an' the littler kids aren't s'posed go there because it was their place—they—they'd go there—smoke an' I guess make love to the girls— They'll kill me, they find out I told—"

"My God in heaven," said Feinman. "Fifteen-year-olds."

"You said it," said Gruber coldly. "The way kids are brought up nowadays. So what can you do to them for it?"

D'Arcy sighed and said, "Not much, Mr. Gruber. But something. Thanks very much for coming in. Freddy, it was brave to tell—it's always better to tell the truth."

"That's all you know!" said Freddy resentfully. "They'll *kill* me!"

D'Arcy and Feinman went up to Le Conte Junior High and located the boys named. The principal and vice-principal, not unbearably surprised, sat in on it. The boys were all big boys for fifteen, and though they used a lot of language which might have surprised their parents, there wasn't much cunning in them and they came apart under some direct questioning, gave the detectives some other names.

"We're going to need some more manpower here," said D'Arcy. "And there'll be all the red tape, damn it." They had to call the parents to notify them that the kids were under arrest. There were about fifteen other kids to locate, six of them girls. Daisy was still in court. Feinman called Sue.

"Oh, *Joe!* I'm in the middle of washing windows and I'm not dressed— Oh, damn!" said Sue. "Why I ever wanted to be a cop— All right, all right, I'll be there as soon as I can!"

The three big boys looked at the detectives defiantly, uneasily, miserably. "Oh, what the hell," said Jerry Noonan, scowling. "So, big deal. It was just a place to go—Walt found out we could get in first—"

"You had the idea—heard your ma say how the old guy'd be gone a long time—"

"Yeah, yeah, we all had the idea—place to go, 's all—with the chicks—an' sometimes we got some pot or speed— You can't say we're holding any now, cop, and what the hell's a little pot? Alla you take a drink—" The tired old argument they all learned to parrot.

"So that's how it started," said D'Arcy. "When? And when did it get to something different?"

"I dunno—it was sometime the middle of last semester, I guess." April? The little house snugly shut up; Czerny wouldn't have known how long he might be away. The water and gas properly shut off. "We went there all last semester. After school and weekends. Once I was there when the guy come to cut the grass"—Jerry laughed loudly—"me and Doris there makin' out and the guy never suspected nothing—I was scared he'd hear us laughin'—"

"It was that damn Wilma," said Walt Altshuler resentfully. "She busted up the toilet that night—"

"Listen, the toilets didn't work anyways," said Jerry. "It was a dumb house—nothin' worked, faucets or nothin'."

"We had some speed that night," said Walt. The kids, of course, liked the speed—Methedrine—because it gave a quick high and a quick down, no results to be noticed by parents. "She was flyin' high and she busted up that toilet, and the rest of us got to—well, it was kind of fun at first. Breaking things up, nobody to know about it—"

"After that, it sort of went on," said Jerry, shrugging. "You know, just kind of a thing to do, we was there. But none of us been back there in a while—it wasn't no fun anymore, no place sit down or make out with the chicks—"

Feinman knew it wasn't any particular use, but he couldn't help it. "Didn't you ever once stop to think that that house was somebody's home?" he said suddenly in a loud voice. "Somebody else's property?" They looked at him blankly, uncomprehendingly. "That all those things meant something to Mr. Czerny?"

There was a little silence, and then Sam Wells said, "Who's Mr. Czerny?"

"Oh, God give me strength," said Feinman.

They were to need it. Sue came in to talk to the girls, who were a good deal more belligerent than the boys. Ellis, Rowan, and Dabney sat in on it, the boys separated into groups. The parents began to descend on them. Maddox and Rodriguez had apparently taken the day off. All this was going to drag on tomorrow and on and on, and it would all be for very little result: the court hearing, possibly a nominal fine, probation, remanded to custody of parents. Some of the parents were as belligerent as the kids; some of them were pained and distressed.

For the moment, the ringleaders—as best they could pick them out—were ferried down to Juvenile Hall, the rest released to the parents. And the paper work there'd be on it—

In the middle of talking to the sullen girls who, incredibly, didn't clearly understand that they'd done anything wrong, Sue was wondering what to get for dinner. Her day off, she'd meant to take time for that special beef stroganoff recipe, but

now—hamburgers, she decided, frozen french fries, and artichoke hearts with lots of butter—that would pacify Ivor—
she'd have to stop for ground beef on her way home.

The answers they heard at the General were probably honest, but not very specific. It was a big place, and very efficient
as a hospital; but it had a large daily turnover of patients, an
enormous staff, and its records were computerized. Maddox
and Rodriguez talked to a lot of people there. They picked up
Ruth Runnels' trail easily, but she wasn't going to be much
help to them when they located her; she was described as
seventy-two and senile. On the complaint of a neighbor, she'd
been found helpless in a single rented room by a sheriff's
deputy in Culver City. They found the helpful Negro nurse
who had bought Aunt Helen's nightgowns and housecoat—
"She was a nice lady, a real lady"—and they prodded the
clerks in the record office with negligible results.

All the records told them was that Ruth Runnels and Helen
Vickers had left the hospital on the same day. Both of them
had had broken hips. Both were to be transferred to the Sunnyvale Convalescent Home. But nobody could tell them what
ambulance service had picked up the patients. An ambulance
had come, as expected. Whence, no one could say.

They even, after patient detective work, tracked down the
two nurse's aides who had taken the patients down to the ambulance entrance. They both said blankly, well, my goodness,
it was just an ambulance. All sorts of private ambulance services; neither had noticed which, and why should they?

It was after five. They went back to Wilcox Street, and into
chaos.

Dick Brougham and Ken Donaldson came onto night watch
at eight o'clock and surveyed the office with interest. Chairs
had been brought in from all over the building and left sitting
at odd angles, all the ashtrays were overflowing, paper cups
with dregs of stale coffee in them were everywhere, and there

was a paper bag on D'Arcy's desk labeled SPEED—DORIS
SIMMS' HANDBAG, 10/1.

"Looks like we missed some action," said Brougham.

"Let's just hope it's a quiet night," said Donaldson.

It was, fairly, until ten o'clock. They had only an attempted
heist at a pharmacy; the pharmacist had pulled a gun and
chased the heister out. They got a description, and Donaldson
said, "Does that ring a bell, Dick? There's an A.P.B. out—"
They looked it up when they got back, and it rang a bell: the
same general description, Donald William Casey, wanted on a
heist last Thursday night. Donaldson typed a report on it.

At ten-forty they got a call from a squad car: a homicide.
They both went out on it. It was Fuller Street below Beverly:
an apartment house.

Patrolman Everard was waiting for them. "The apartment
manager found it—Mr. Hopkins. These are the detectives,
sir."

"Never had such a shock," said Hopkins, panting at them.
He was a fat old man in a frayed bathrobe over slacks and
T-shirt. "It's the first of the month and he owed me rent, and
I hadn't noticed him coming or going for a few days, so I went
up, try to catch him. Third-floor back, he had. No answer to
the bell. Then I noticed there was this big stain on the carpet
from under the door—got to looking, and there was more
stains all along the hall and stairs—so I used my key, and oh,
lordy, there he was—all over blood—so I called the police and
the officer says he's been shot—"

He certainly seemed to have been shot, a powder-burned
hole in his shirt in the middle of his chest. He was lying on his
back just inside the door, and he'd been dead for quite a
while.

"What's his name?" asked Brougham.

"Berry—Peter J. Berry. Just a young guy, you can see. He
lived here about two years, usually paid the rent on time, till
the last couple months. Never had any trouble with him, wild
parties or nothing. How d'you figure he coulda got shot?"
asked Hopkins plaintively.

CHAPTER 7

Thursday was supposed to be Maddox' day off. But there'd
be miles of red tape on the kids, and he was interested in following up the Sunnyvale thing—he went in. It would just get
added to the days they owed him, and maybe sometime he
and Sue would want to take a vacation.

The first thing he found, of course, was the night-watch report on the new homicide. He said this and that about it.
Feinman, Ellis, and Rowan came in and took Sue right out
with them, downtown to Juvenile Hall; they'd be back to get
on with the paper work. Rodriguez was reading the homicide
report and saying that was all they needed when Peasmarsh
called.

"I thought you should be informed that the district attorney's office has issued a warrant on the Parks woman. Com-
mendably, they do like to get right on these cases. We'd be
obliged if you execute it as soon as possible. I have seen your
excellent witness Mrs. Vickers, by the way. She certainly gives
us some clear-cut evidence. However, I've also been in touch
with the General hospital, and a number of the other former
patients can be interviewed sometime today."

Maddox said, "We're a little shorthanded here, but we'll try
to get on it."

"I should like to, er, sit in on that if you don't mind—
perhaps we could meet at the hospital, say at one o'clock?"

"I don't know. If this warrant—well, all right, I'll see somebody's there by then."

Peasmarsh rang off and Maddox said, "Damnation. Talk
about quick off the mark—just as well to get Parks in jail, but
we can't do everything at once."

Dabney came in and said, "Sorry I'm late—I did set the alarm, but I was pooped. Have you noticed the new homicide? I like it."

"Did Dick and Ken get you out of bed?" asked Rodriguez. "They would."

"What else? There wasn't much we could do, but we had to get photos of the corpse before the morgue wagon came. Then we just sealed the place and left it. But I was interested enough that I came on back to develop the negs and make prints." He had just picked up the dried prints on his way up. Maddox took the sheaf of glossy eight-by-tens and after a minute said, "I'll be damned." He passed the first one on to Rodriguez, studied the next. "I will be— Am I reading this right?"

"Yep," said Dabney through a yawn. "What they call instant retribution."

Maddox laughed. The stark candid shots showed the body of a man lying full-length on his back just inside an open door. He was a young man, with a round clean-shaven face and fair hair; a pair of horn-rimmed glasses had fallen off his nose and lay beside one shoulder. There was a darkened roundish mark in the middle of his chest; he was wearing a plaid shirt and dark pants. There was a good deal of blood on his clothes, the carpet nearby. Just above his head a large paper bag had broken open and a miscellany of articles spilled from it: a pair of silver candlesticks, a flat velvet box, a little wad of crumpled paper money half hidden by a fur stole.

"I recognized the plaid shirt," said Dabney. "I told you he left a sizable piece torn off on the screen door. If we can get anybody to identify the loot, it'll be from the Peller woman's house. The rest of it'll be enough in the way of evidence anyway—we got casts of the footprints, and he was wearing the same shoes, and the shirt fragment'll match up too. I saw the lab picked out some more prints—wonder if they're his. If so, he hadn't any record."

"I will be damned," said Rodriguez, amused. "So she did wing him—and in a vital spot, if not immediately. Where was this? . . . Fuller Street—that'd only be a block or so away, Ivor. He managed to get home, probably not realizing he was hit so bad, just got inside the apartment and *finis*. That's a queer one."

"Also a stupid one, if we read it right and he broke into the house sometime that afternoon," said Dabney. "The clincher will be the slug, I told the morgue to send it to the lab but that won't be till the autopsy. They've got her gun. If the slugs match, which I've got no doubt they will, there'll be just a report to write."

"And an inquest, and next of kin to notify," said Maddox. "The shortcuts are always helpful." Pending the arrival of that warrant, he and Rodriguez went over to the apartment on Fuller Street to look around. The only evidence of the corpse was the blood on the carpet, outside in the hall, a great dark patch where he had died. Dabney had brought his little loot in last night. It was a rather pathetically bare little apartment, not many clothes in the closet, not much food in the refrigerator, no amenities of decor added to the bare furnishings. Beside the phone in the bedroom they found an address book. Under B was listed a Joan Berry, address in Lakewood. "Next of kin to Peter? We'd better ask."

He dialed the number and was presently answered by a sleepy voice; he introduced himself and as diplomatically as possible explained why he was calling. The voice ceased to sound sleepy.

"You're a close relative, Miss Berry? I'm very sorry to have to—"

"His sister," she said numbly. "Oh, my God. No—it's all right, I know you have to— I'd better come, hadn't I?"

"We'll have to get the body formally identified, but if there's anyone else who can do that—his father or—"

"There's nobody," she said. "I'll come. Where? Right now?"

"Wilcox Street Police Station. Could you make it by eleven o'clock?"

"I'll be there," she said. "And thank you for letting me know."

"Damnation," said Maddox, "there's another appointment." At least there wasn't much for them to do on this one; it was finished as soon as it started. And it cleared up the Peller homicide. "Just as I said at the time, somebody in the neighborhood who'd heard the rumor, third or fourth hand, old

Mrs. Peller had a lot of money—not a very bright somebody, Peter Berry, if he expected it to be in the house—breaking in to look for it, and she met him with the gun."

When they got back to Wilcox Street the warrant on Rose Parks had just come through, but nobody else was there and they had to hang around to talk to Joan Berry. They tossed a quarter and Rodriguez lost so he got busy on a report on Berry. Just before he finished it D'Arcy came in looking morose and said he'd decided, even if he ever got married, he never wanted to see a kid again in his life. "Lot of worthless little bastards," he said, sitting down at his desk and rolling a report form into the typewriter. "I don't say our generation were all angels, but my God, at that age I never even knew some of the language they throw around."

"Whether they can spell it or not," said Maddox wryly. "At least we've just got two birds killed with one stone." D'Arcy was interested in that, and delayed his report while he heard about it. "What a silly bastard," he said, "trying a break-in in broad daylight—he might have known the old lady was there."

"Maybe his best gamble," said Maddox. "Old ladies aren't very often out at night. She could have been out shopping or something—and it was raining, not likely he'd be seen or heard by neighbors."

Rodriguez finished the report, slapped it together and stapled it, and lit a cigarette. "The seven o'clock news said we're going to have more rain, isn't that ducky?"

"Sergeant Maddox?" said a hesitant voice from the door, and they looked up.

"You'll be Miss Berry? Come in. I'm Maddox. Detective Rodriguez—Detective D'Arcy. I was very sorry to have to break such bad news to you, Miss Berry." She was a nice-looking young woman, short wiry blond hair, a fresh clear complexion, a rather square face with candid hazel eyes now clouded with sorrow. She had a good, if rather sturdy, figure in navy suit and white blouse.

"It couldn't be helped," she said, taking the offered chair. "How—how did it happen? I know Peter had a gun—did—he didn't shoot himself, did he?"

"No. I'm afraid this will be another shock to you, but—"

Maddox explained at a little length, and she sat huddled in the chair, nodding silently. At last she opened her bag and took out a cigarette; he held out his lighter, but D'Arcy lunged between them with his.

"Thanks. I—oh, my God," said Joan Berry, "I can only be thankful, Mother and Dad are gone, not to know. Peter—doing a damn fool thing like that. He could have come to me. I know he'd been worried at being out of work. He—oh, I might as well admit it, he wasn't the smartest man around— but he was kind and good and— He was just about at the end of the unemployment compensation, I know he'd been worried. It wasn't as if he could take any old job that called for a strong back—he was no good with his hands, and he had rheumatic fever when he was seven, his heart wasn't strong. I—oh, damn," she said, and groped for a handkerchief.

"Have some Kleenex," said D'Arcy rather hoarsely.

"Thanks." She wiped her eyes. "But to try a burglary—he must have been really feeling desperate—"

"Did you say he had a gun, Miss Berry? We didn't come across one."

"He'd probably pawned it. And anything else he could. I didn't know he was that low—when I talked with him on the phone, it was a week ago last night—oh, lord, I should have kept in closer touch, I usually did, but I was in bed three days with a miserable cold—anyway, he said he had some savings, he'd be all right. He ought to have come to me, he knew I'd help him out—at least I've got a steady job—"

"Where?" asked D'Arcy.

"At the phone company, I'm on a split shift mostly at night —the reason I wasn't exactly on all cylinders when you called, Sergeant. I'm sorry, you're not interested in that. You said I—have to identify him?"

"Isn't there somebody else could do that?" asked D'Arcy. She shook her head. "I'll take you down then. You needn't be afraid, not really such an ordeal."

"I've seen bodies before," she said wearily. But she wouldn't be looking forward to it.

D'Arcy looked vaguely at Maddox and Rodriguez and said he'd be back after a while. He helped her on with her coat tenderly and ushered her out. "Must be a terrible shock to you, but we'll do all we can to make it easier, Miss Berry—you do realize there'll have to be an autopsy, pure formality, but I'll let you know as soon as you can get on to arranging the services—watch those stairs, they're tricky—"

Maddox and Rodriguez looked at each other. "Well, I said it was too good to be true," said Rodriguez. "It was bound to happen. He's in love again."

"She seems like an ordinary nice girl, but nothing spectacular, looks or any other way. Of course she's a blonde," said Maddox.

"I don't think he'll make much headway there," said Rodriguez.

"Why not?"

"Well," said Rodriguez reasonably, "how on earth are they ever going to get together, when she's working nights?"

Maddox laughed. "Leave it to D'Arcy's ingenuity. Come on, we've got to go arrest this female."

The only address they had for Rose Parks was the old Victorian monstrosity on Vermont; evidently she'd been living there. They found the front door open, and went in to curious echoes of their footsteps in the high-ceilinged rooms, empty of life now. The cobwebs swung lazily in the corners; the smells remained, faintly. Dust rose under their feet.

"She's run," said Rodriguez. "She knew there'd likely be a charge."

"It was a gamble—and she couldn't have expected us so soon." They poked around the rambling first floor. There were mounds of dirty laundry heaped on a square back porch; the gloomy old-fashioned kitchen was crowded with stacks of dirty dishes, spoiling food. "Good place for ghosts," said Maddox. The place felt enormous about them, being empty. They climbed stairs. On the second floor were more empty, dirty rooms, more litter and dust and cobwebs.

"If she's here she's heard us by now."

She had. As they turned down a cross hall at the rear, Maddox caught one light, cautious footfall at the front; they whirled and caught up with her just skipping down the front stairs. "No, you didn't expect us so soon, did you?" said Maddox. "We have a warrant for your arrest, Mrs. Parks."

She stood there silent, giving no sign of regret at having lost the gamble: an ugly angular woman, her long bucktoothed face impassive. She had apparently made quick preparations to run, hearing them come in; she held an overnight bag in one hand, a fat handbag in the other; she was wearing a heavy wool coat over a dark dress. "What's the charge?" she asked in a flat voice.

"To start with, aggravated assault."

She just nodded. Maddox left her with Rodriguez while he went up to the top floor and found the room she'd been living in. It was cleaner than any of the others, clean sheets on the bed, no cobwebs. He had a quick look around, but there was nothing there except clothes; if there had existed any more papers, any more concrete evidence useful to them, it had been disposed of.

The only car parked in the front yard was registered to her, a ten-year-old Ford; Maddox called the police garage to tow it in for examination.

She was silent all the way down to the Alameda jail. There, she was booked in and printed, and the clerk made out a receipt for the personal belongings taken from her. And they were extremely interesting. In the overnight case were clothes, new and expensive clothes, strangely feminine and lacy nightgowns, a smart blue pantsuit, new underclothes, cosmetics. In the fat black handbag was her wallet, with a hundred dollars in it; and crammed into the zippered compartment at the back, ten thousand dollars in crisp new paper money.

They waited for the kickback from NCIC; with all the computers, it didn't take long. Her prints were not known to be on file anywhere; she hadn't any pedigree under any name.

Maddox went to call Peasmarsh, and then he and Rodriguez went out to lunch.

Sue came back to the station after a belated lunch, intending to get through her last stint of the paper work on the juveniles. Today should about wind it up; there was no telling when the court hearing might be scheduled—sometime next week or the week after—and she didn't think it was going to corrupt those kids to be rubbing shoulders with kids a little tougher down at Juvenile Hall in the meantime. She just hoped getting caught up to had scared them a little, but she wouldn't take a bet on it.

But she got deflected. She visited the rest room, freshened lipstick and tidied her hair, and had just come out again when a messenger from downtown brought up a couple of reports. There wasn't anybody else in; she looked, and one was the autopsy report on Pauline, the other a lab report, surprisingly bulky. She read the autopsy report first.

Pauline had died, very quickly, of manual strangulation, the hyoid bone crushed. It was an easy way to kill somebody, without meaning to; she thought speculatively of Bill Blackwell's wide shoulders and big hands. He wouldn't be the first man to lose his temper with a silly importunate female, and five minutes later find he'd killed her. Thursday night—the autopsy gave it a leeway between 10 P.M. and 6 A.M., but they knew it had to be after eleven— And he had gone back to the Ledbetters' with the hamburgers. When he left, then—a gamble, leaving the body in his car until then, but it would have been one, one-thirty, not much later; he had to be in class the next morning. Twenty minutes to drive up Mulholland, toss her over the hillside. Pauline—"a sweet kid, and I love her"—but self-preservation, unlike death, was stronger than love.

The only other item the autopsy offered was that Pauline had died a virgin. She hadn't been beaten.

Sue opened the other manila envelope and a box slid out. That had been the bulk; the report was a handful of nothing, on their investigation of the clothes and so on. Nothing under her fingernails; she'd been taken by surprise, then, no time to fight back. There was nothing to be had from her clothes, sodden with rain over that entire weekend. The report concluded noncommittally that the personal effects from the body were included; unless there was a specific request for the clothes they would be destroyed.

Sue sighed. Sometimes, not often but oftener than they liked, a case like this came along, where they were morally sure who X was but had no way to prove it. She opened the

box, which was fastened with tape, and looked at a few pieces
of jewelry. A class ring from Hollywood High, ten-karat gold
with a fake ruby. A silver and turquoise ring. A pair of stud
earrings for pierced ears, silver and turquoise. A sterling
pendant, a replica of a sand dollar, on a slender sterling chain.

She called the Strange house and got Mrs. Strange, and told
her that they could claim the body; that Pauline's jewelry
could be claimed at any time.

"Oh, yes—we want that. Thank you, we'll— You—you
haven't found out yet—what did happen?"

"We're still investigating, Mrs. Strange," A few more reports, she thought, and shove it in Pending. Unless Bill's conscience bothered him, or he could be leaned on hard enough
to break him down. Sue dwelt one by one on the nice, amiable, polite detectives at Wilcox Street, from her easygoing
spouse to sardonic suave Rodriguez, to friendly, soft-voiced
Feinman, to serious-minded Rowan, philosophic Dabney, to
moody D'Arcy—really the only one of them who even looked
like a big tough cop was George Ellis, and he was soft as butter inside. Not that she really wanted to turn back the clock to
when cops used the third degree, but if Bill could be con-
vinced they might, conceivably he'd come out with the truth.

She heard Feinman and D'Arcy coming up the stairs.
"Honestly, Joe, the minute I saw her—there's just something
about her, I can't explain it—something, you know, sort of
wholesome. She hasn't had an easy time either, she told me a
little—I bought her a cup of coffee downtown—had to work
all through high school, her father dead, and her mother died
just last year—and now losing her brother too, if he was a stupid bastard. Honestly, you can tell, a special sort of girl—and
I never knew a blonde with hazel eyes before—"

D'Arcy had apparently fallen in love again. Sue wondered
who it was this time, and if he'd ever settle down for good
with one girl.

She had just finished the last report at five forty-five and
said, "Oof! Thank heaven that's that," when a little wind
swept against the window and brought a splatter with it. She
looked up. It had begun to rain again. And a moment later
Mr. and Mrs. Strange came up the stairs.

Sue handed over the box, and Mrs. Strange choked back a

sob, taking it. "Please," said her husband, "I know when you said about—being able to have the body now—it means the—the autopsy—"

"Yes, sir, that's right."

Mrs. Strange said in a low voice, not looking up, "Can you tell us if she—if she—"

"No, she wasn't raped," said Sue gently.

"Oh. Thank you." She opened the box and fingered the jewelry. "Her class ring— But that's not hers. That necklace."

"Are you sure?" Sue was surprised.

"Oh, yes. She couldn't abide things made in the shape of creepy-crawlie things like that. I never saw it before in my life. It isn't Sylvia's either." Mrs. Strange laid it on the desk. "Where'd it come from?"

Sue looked back over the lab report. The necklace had been in the pocket of the coral pantsuit. "Maybe it belonged to one of her girl friends—"

"I don't know," said Mrs. Strange. "It's funny. That pantsuit was brand-new, it was the first time she'd worn it."

Maddox came out the front entrance of the General hospital with Rodriguez and stood on the top step, sniffing deeply of the newly rain-laden air. "Hospitals," he said. It was nearly dark.

"And people," said Rodriguez. "Thank God it's my day off tomorrow."

They hadn't had to call on headquarters for additional manpower yet; Peasmarsh had brought along a couple of men from his office. Among them they'd talked to twelve of the patients fetched out of that hellhole last Tuesday, and got a lot more corroborating evidence.

One of the first Maddox had talked to was the gray old man they'd seen in the wheelchair just before Aunt Helen was rescued last Monday. He was clean-shaven now, in clean hospital gown and robe, and talking coherently if a little weakly. His name was Edward Munsing. He'd gone into the hospital last February for a prostate operation, and the doctor told him he'd better spend a few weeks in a convalescent home, till he got back on his feet. He was a widower without any family, living on his Social Security and a little pension from his old job paid into his bank every month; he got by, he said, living in a rented room over on Fourth. Used to sit in the park and feed the pigeons, talk to other people there. But he didn't know anybody, now, close enough to want to come to see him, wonder where he was. He said that Parks woman used to give him shots, maybe tranquilizers—kept him all doped up, so he couldn't think straight, get up the strength to try to get out of that place. He couldn't believe yet that he was out of it, and nothing much wrong with him at all, as soon as he got his strength back. The doctor said he could leave in a few days. "And I got no idea where all my stuff'd be—all my clothes, everything I had—I suppose the landlady took it when I didn't come back, I just hope she's kept it all."

There was an old lady named Ella Jones, nearly eighty, who was crippled with rheumatoid arthritis but still very much there mentally, who was mightily enjoying all the attention paid her by the nurses and now the nice policemen. She'd have gone on talking all night, and she enlarged on the iniquities of Mrs. Parks and her staff, giving details that made Peasmarsh very happy. She was a widow; she'd had a son and a daughter, but the son had been killed in the Second World War and the daughter, unmarried, had died in an accident almost two years ago. Mrs. Jones just had her Social Security, and after that, with nobody to take care of her, she'd had to go to a rest home. She'd been in the hospital, yes, this one here, after the daughter was killed—"Such a terrible shock it was, just imagine Corinne going before me, and I knew I'd have to give up the apartment, she was in a good job and supported us both— But once I got into that place, you can see I couldn't get out— Ooh, how I hated that Parks woman! The things she did—all of them—to all of us—I don't know why I'm still alive!"

There was Mr. and Mrs. Clyde Burrows, eighty-one and eighty-five respectively, who didn't quite know how they'd got to Mrs. Parks' home. They were definite that they'd been in a nice, clean, comfortable convalescent home at first. It had got to be too much for them to keep up the house, the yard; they both had arthritis and weak hearts. They'd never had any chil-

dren, and all their relatives were dead. They'd sold the house
and paid all the money to a home run by some religious
group, with the understanding that they'd be taken care of the
rest of their lives. But at some time, they didn't know just
when, they'd found themselves in Mrs. Parks' tender hands.

There was Howard Trumbull, an old bachelor retired from
long years in the merchant marine. "Never did believe in
gatherin' moss," he told Rodriguez. "Always make new friends
around the next corner—somehow never did keep in touch
with old ones. You never think—you never think how it's gonna
be—when you get old and can't move on anymore." He was a
diabetic, and had to go into the hospital to have a leg
amputated, gangrene in it. He'd been living in a single room
down in San Pedro, where he could watch the ships every
day, but the doctors said he'd have to go to a rest home for a
while anyway. "I never did expect to enjoy it," he said surlily.
He also gave chapter and verse, about the indignities, the lack
of attention, the cheap unappetizing food, the threats and
blows and occasional hypos if you complained or made any
noise.

They had seen Ruth Runnels, and of course she was no use
to them at all: a fat, vague-eyed old woman drooling at the
mouth, senile and silent. The nurse told them she might not
live long, her heart was bad.

Peasmarsh had got a lot more nice evidence. Peasmarsh, of
course, was single-mindedly concerned to slap a stiff charge
and sentence on Mrs. Parks and hopefully on her staff as well.
He had now discovered that she'd never had a license to operate the home, never even applied for one.

"They were all people alone," said Maddox now, lighting a
cigarette. "Without anybody to take any note of what happened to them. All those we talked to, at least. I'd expect, all
of them period."

"It'd have to be that way," said Rodriguez. "She couldn't
have kept it up otherwise. Or, of course, people whose nearest
and dearest didn't give a damn—and there are some like that
too. Grandpa starts to go senile, shove him out of sight in a
rest home, who's to be bothered going to see him."

"Yes. And of course she was paying out as little as possible
in overhead, raking in the Social Security and I suppose the

Medicare payments—indigent old people— But where," asked Maddox, "did Aunt Helen come in? And Miss Runnels?"

"Aunt Helen," said Rodriguez through a yawn, "is kind of obvious. They thought nobody cared about her either, and then the Fosters came battering in the door and they had to try to cover up. And I could suggest an explanation for that rigmarole with Mrs. Cleveland too—I wonder what her first name is."

"The explanation I'd like to hear."

"Just as I said, the Parks woman is caught with Aunt Helen. She, or the ambulance attendants, or somebody at the General, had mislabeled the two women and she hadn't realized it until the Fosters came barging in. She knew they'd be back, though she didn't expect police—more probably a lawyer—but she knew if any outsider got more than a glimpse of that place she'd soon be out of business. She had to get Aunt Helen out of there, be able to shoo the Fosters off on the doorstep by telling them where she was. And she knew the Cleveland woman."

"From where?"

"They're both registered nurses," pointed out Rodriguez, "if one of them was nominally in a high-class job and the other one wasn't. Maybe they trained at the same place—maybe they'd worked together years ago. And just maybe Parks has a hold on her, and that wouldn't surprise me. There's more to Cleveland than goodness-gracious-see-what-a-lady-I-am. I wouldn't put anything past that one, and a lot more subtle than Parks. Sex or money, and if the edge is on money it's only just. God knows what Parks might have on her that'd put her out of a good job and maybe defrock her of the R.N. degree. Anyway, Parks calls and yells for help. She puts Aunt Helen out with morphine, probably Cleveland came right over with her own car, they bundled her out, and Cleveland gets her up to the other place. Gets her cleaned up and looking cared for. And Cleveland keeps her staff on its toes, she wears the pants there. I can't guess what tale she might have told them, but part of the story she told us would be as good as anything—terrible mistake in names, black eye for the whole profession, relatives irate, better smooth it all down or it might get into the papers and cause a lot of trouble—so,

back her up that Aunt Helen'd been there all along. Or maybe
it was just, play up or lose your job. Pay your money and take
your choice," said Rodriguez.

"It's your story. I could buy it," said Maddox. "I could indeed. It'd be nice to get her to admit it—unless we do, that
tale would discredit Aunt Helen's evidence, not that Peasmarsh really needs it now. Yes, I could buy that. Because for
one thing, being a normal red-blooded male, I'm aware that
Cleveland is anything but an ice maiden."

"*¡Pues hombre!*" said Rodriguez. "*Sin mujeres y sin celos, no
hay de consuelo.* Without women or hunger, no pleasure."

"But what worries me," said Maddox, "is the names. Why
were the names changed, César? Somebody did that deliberately, and Aunt Helen says it was Parks. Why?"

Rodriguez said, "Are we going home tonight? Yes, I see
what you mean. It's just an odd little thing."

"Peasmarsh has got his case all wrapped up, and the deputy D.A.'ll be pleased. But it was Aunt Helen who started the
whole thing, and I can't make out how she landed there. How
any of them landed there, for that matter— You know what I
come up with. There's got to be a link to the General. They all
—well, we aren't sure, but all of them we've talked to—
started out at the General. There must have been somebody
there—aide, orderly, clerk—recruiting patients for Parks. The
ones with nobody to care what happened to them, safe game."

"It's a premise," said Rodriguez, shrugging. "I'm going
home. Good night."

"It'd be interesting to know who," said Maddox. "And I'd
like to locate that ambulance too." He watched Rodriguez
move off toward the parking lot, tossed his cigarette away,
and started after him.

Halfway home he remembered that he ought to have called
that lieutenant in Pittsburgh, asked him to inform Mrs.
Peller's niece that she could now claim the body and pay for a
funeral. Come to think, he'd better pass on Barton's name for
her; Barton could do all the clearing up for her.

Sue had veal parmigiana and baked potatoes, the rest of the

artichoke hearts. "If I ever decide to stay home and be a housewife, you might get something besides things out of the freezer."

"No complaints," said Maddox. But he was preoccupied; he wandered around the little house while she did the dishes. The rain slithered down outside, gentle as yet. "There is something," he said, leaning on the refrigerator watching her, "nagging at me, just on the tip of my subconscious mind, and I don't know what the hell it is."

"Stop trying and it'll come to you."

"Why in hell were the names changed? A link to the General—and Cleveland—I wonder what her first name is indeed—mmh, yes. The original ice maiden—I don't think. Gloria. Alexandra. Christabel. All very suitable," said Maddox. "But Parks? Bucktoothed Parks? Well, they needn't ever have been buddies if Parks just had a hold. From someplace they'd worked together. We could follow Parks back, I suppose. But is it necessary? Damn it, if I could just think of what's trying to get through to me—if I could get a line on that ambulance —" Evidently no record kept at the General of which ambulance came for whom; possibly the ambulance attendants could tell them which aide or orderly gave them directions where to go. A lot of ambulance services in the country, but not an astronomical number. They could probably chase it down in time, a lot of time.

"I think," he said suddenly, "I'd like to talk to Aunt Helen again."

"If it'll stop you fidgeting around like this, go," said Sue. "You with your detective problem and me with mine. Only I hope I've learned not to bring the office home."

Peasmarsh had said he'd talked with Aunt Helen. "Your excellent witness." And added that she had left the hospital and was at home. Maddox got out his raincoat again and drove over to LaClede Street in the Atwater district.

He found them all cozily ensconced before a fire in the hearth, drinking hot cocoa. "Now isn't this nice," said Myra Foster hospitably, "do come in and sit down, Sergeant. There's plenty on the stove, I'll get you a cup." Maddox didn't remember drinking hot cocoa since high school and night football games; it tasted nostalgic.

"I'm glad you're able to be out of the hospital, Mrs. Vickers."

"Oh, I'm going to be fine. We rented that thing"—she nodded at the steel walker in one corner—"and I can get along pretty good with it already, the doctor thought inside a month I'd be able to do without it."

"What's going on about that place?" asked Leo Foster curiously. "We had a fellow here from the Board of Health, very energetic little guy—" It described Peasmarsh.

Maddox told them that Mrs. Parks was in jail. "Well, I'm very happy to hear that!" said Myra emphatically. He didn't tell them the story Mrs. Cleveland had come out with. There'd have been fireworks at that, if he knew Myra and Aunt Helen.

The fat black cat sauntered in and jumped up on Aunt Helen's lap and she stroked him. "He's never seen snow, have you, Sammy? I wonder how he'll like it."

"Oh, our old Tiger used to love it," said Myra.

Maddox opened his mouth to say that Mrs. Vickers' testimony would probably be wanted at the trial, and desisted. If Cleveland stuck to that story, Peasmarsh might decide not to befuddle the judge's mind with Aunt Helen. "Could you tell me," he asked, "it doesn't seem to have come up—just exactly how did you come to pick that particular convalescent home? Was it recommended to you, or what? A nurse's aide? How was it arranged?"

"Why, it just sort of came about," said Aunt Helen. She looked like another woman than the one he'd first seen, unconscious in the hospital bed: her gray hair curled in a gay upsweep, her alert thin face delicately colored with cosmetics; she didn't look within ten years of her age. "When they said first I'd have to go into a convalescent home, I thought right off of the one Alida James was in after her stroke—it was a nice place, so clean and bright, and she said everyone was so nice—Chapman's it was out in West Hollywood, and I mentioned it to the nurse. Not wait a minute," she said suddenly. "They gave me a list—one of the regular nurses, I think it was, and everybody said most of the places were good and I'd be satisfied with any one I picked, but they were usually pretty crowded and it would probably be a question of finding one with space. And I suppose it was the office at the hospital that checked on that, anyway the day before, one of the nurses told me they'd found a place for me at this Sunnyvale home. It sounded like a nice place, and I was pleased to see it was right in Hollywood, closer to home than some of the others." She laughed. "What was in my mind was the ambulance fee to get home again, which was silly, because that'd all be taken care of by the Medicare."

"Yes," said Maddox. All that didn't pinpoint anybody. If it suggested anything, it suggested some anonymous clerk in the office at the hospital. "Well, thanks anyway," he said despondently, finishing his cocoa.

The L.A.P.D. ran two-man cars in the high-crime areas. Patrolmen Keeler and Rinehart were cruising down Avalon about ten o'clock that night; there wasn't much traffic, in the rain, and they were discussing politics when Rinehart said, "Look at that damn fool!" A car in the next lane ahead of them, doing at least forty, hit a pond of water in a dip and veered half around with a screech of brakes, bouncing off the center divider. It backed out, and Keeler had to stand on the brake to save the squad car's nose. The car shot off weaving from lane to lane, and Rinehart got on the mike. "K14, in pursuit of a 502, Avalon and Fifty-ninth."

"All cars, K14 is in pursuit of a 502—"

They caught up with it six blocks later, curbed it, and got the driver out. There wasn't any need to give him an on-the-street test; he was falling-down drunk, it was just lucky he hadn't killed somebody. In fact, he passed out as they were trying to get an I.D. from him. Rinehart looked at him disgustedly as he lay there on the street in the rain, and then he said suddenly, "Hey, Johnny, there was an A.P.B. out on a guy matches his description—" They got a wallet from his pants and found I.D.—Social Security, National Auto Club—Donald William Casey, the A.P.B. said wanted for a heist job. They called the plate number in and found it was a stolen car.

They called headquarters and took him down to the Alameda jail, to be stashed in the drunk tank for the night and turned over to the front-office boys later.

CHAPTER 8

It was sprinkling slightly on Friday morning. Maddox, D'Arcy, and Feinman came in together just before Ellis, Dabney, and Rowan; they had a look at the night-watch report. So Casey had been picked up, fine, but now somebody would have to go downtown and book him into jail on the warrant, maybe get a statement from him. There had also been two more heist jobs, one at a drugstore, one at a supermarket, and a woman had been mugged on Cahuenga Boulevard; she'd been sent to the hospital, unconscious, and somebody would have to see her, find out her name and anything she could tell.

D'Arcy went to do that, and Feinman to see Casey. Daisy was still downtown in court, and already a trio of distressed parents—there had been a few left over, not talked to yet, from the juvenile case—had arrived and been shunted off to Sue. Maddox heard just one wail: "But she's never been in any trouble before!" Donaldson had appended a note; the drugstore owner would be in at one o'clock to make a statement. It looked like being a busy day.

He was about to take off when Peasmarsh called him. "I thought you'd like to know that Mrs. Parks is to be indicted at ten A.M."

"Well, the D.A. got right at this one," said Maddox, surprised.

"We like to make an example of these cases. There's no need for you to appear, I'll be there to offer evidence. But the deputy and I aren't just clear whether there's sufficient evidence to bring a charge against the employees, I haven't interviewed them at all. If you could do so—"

"I was just going out to chase them up."

"Very good," said Peasmarsh. "I'll be hearing from you then."

Maddox put the phone down and it shrilled at him again. This time it was the D.A.'s office. Rex Slaney was to be indicted this morning; after due deliberation, they were reducing the charge to involuntary manslaughter, and not charging Mrs. Thomas at all.

Maddox said this and that; but his job was to catch up to them, and he couldn't do anything about it when the courts accepted a whitewashed plea.

He had the addresses from Peasmarsh; he went out and wasted the morning talking to Rose Parks' erstwhile staff.

The Kleppers, Fred and Gerda, he found in a bare, chilly apartment on Berendo Street. They were in their early thirties, a stolid fair couple, immigrants of two years ago; their papers, obediently produced, were in order. He thought irrelevantly of Anton Czerny. "*Ja*, the business is close down," said Klepper. "We know. We work there nearly two year. Not too bad pay."

Had they ever considered the patients to be mistreated?— noticed the blows, threats?—thought the staff too small for the number of patients? Gerda Klepper said indifferently, "Old people like children—nuisance to look to, but have to make rules."

"*Ja*." He nodded. "Hard work, look to the old peoples. We get easier job next."

Robert Pine, living in an old house in Bellflower with his mother and a brother, was just a simple-minded lout with a strong back; at any job he held, and there wouldn't be many he could do, he'd just obey whatever orders were given him. When Maddox asked him whether he thought the old people were treated roughly, he just stared and said, "I done what she told me, that's all."

At a ramshackle bungalow on Boyd Street, in downtown L.A., he didn't succeed in communicating with Anita Arrubes much at all; her English was strictly limited. It would, of course, be César's day off. "*¿Qué es esto? No se, no se.*" Hordes of Arrubes were present; an older sister translated for her in a thick accent. "She say, all old people were crazy, no sense waste pity, good food on. Too hard job, she don't like. She don't take such job again."

Maddox came back to the office and found D'Arcy telling

Sue all about his new lady love. "Oh, and Casey was still in the throes of a hangover. I didn't try to get anything out of him, we've got him tied up tight anyway."

"At least," said Sue, "we've got all the paper work cleaned up on the juveniles. If you ask me, paper work is the curse of the twentieth century."

Maddox sat down at his desk and called Peasmarsh; it was after twelve, but possibly Peasmarsh the dedicated civil servant ate a sandwich at his desk. At any rate, he was there. "If you want my considered opinion," said Maddox, "you wouldn't get anywhere charging Parks' staff. They're just unimaginative little people minus any rudimentary sympathy for anybody else. I don't know whether you've noticed, but there aren't many brother's keepers around nowadays."

"I see," said Peasmarsh. "I rather thought it would turn out that way. I just got back from court. The judge ordered her held on fifty thousand bail."

"Gratifying," said Maddox. Putting the phone down, he got out those two shabby items that were all the so-called records Peasmarsh had found in that place and had a closer look at them. It wasn't very enlightening. The ordinary dime-store tablet was half-filled with penciled lists of names: just surnames. Patients, he deduced, recognizing some as belonging to some of the people they'd seen yesterday. Just names, no attempt at cataloguing illnesses, diet, medication. Some of the names were crossed out: when they had died? Not necessarily. Here was, at the very end of the list, *Runnels* with a firm line though it. He half grinned at that. This looked like a bare list of what people were actually in the house. But of course it was in the cards that there'd been a lot more evidence there, records of Medicare receipts and so on, that she'd had time to destroy. Peasmarsh and his men had gone in to look at the place and then had to wait a few hours for the court order.

The address book was, if possible, even more uninformative; it didn't contain any addresses at all, only phone numbers. Just eleven phone numbers, with only single initials attached. D. NO 1-6494. G. SP 2-5408. F. MA 4-8496. P. HO 7-8399. J. RE 3-7904. And so on. He puzzled over them awhile. They looked like legitimate phone numbers, not a crude cipher of any kind. The prefixes were all kosher: Normandie, Lorain, Madison, Hollywood, Republic. The others were farther afield. All they told him was that Parks was a little old-fashioned, putting down the numbers with letter prefixes instead of all numbers.

He got the office of the phone company and asked for a rundown on all of them, matching addresses. Police business. He gave the girl the desk number and the office number. It might be interesting to see who Rose Parks' friends were.

He went up to the Grotto on Santa Monica Boulevard and found Feinman, Sue, and D'Arcy already there.

"I don't think we'll get much on that other heist," said D'Arcy. "Anonymous. Two thugs in stocking masks caught the assistant manager of the market as he was closing up, right at the door. The parking lot was empty at midnight, no witnesses. The manager had a gun, and they exchanged shots, but the thugs got away with the loot. But a funny little thing showed up—Rowan's still there looking around—one slug went through the door of the beauty shop next door to the market, the owner hadn't even noticed it when she opened up. We traced it. It's not damaged at all, ricocheted off the wall and went into a plastic chair—and Joe wants to see if it's out of the manager's gun. He doesn't think so and neither do I. The manager had a .22 and this looks more like a .25. Anyway, we'd have a ballistics sample to hang on to."

"For what it's worth," muttered Maddox.

Sue said she wanted to talk to Bill Blackwell again. "Not that I think we could scare him. I wish we could. He's really the only answer, on Pauline."

"I don't know that we want to scare him," said Feinman seriously. "He's a good type. If it was him, and that's the way it spells out easiest, we'll have his conscience working for us. I want to see him again too." They went on talking about it, and D'Arcy bored Maddox with some more enthusiasm about Joan Berry.

They got back to the office about one o'clock and found Rowan there talking with a middle-aged citizen: the owner of the drugstore that had been held up last night. His name was Dangerfield. Rowan looked hungry, and Maddox said he and D'Arcy would take over.

"Not the first time I've been held up, they're after the pills, you know," said Dangerfield. "Though this one wasn't, he never went near the pharmacy. I guess you'll want a description. He was a young fellow about six feet, medium build, brown hair, and he was halfway drunk when he came in. One reason I wasn't about to tangle with him, man in that condition waving a gun around—"

"Oh, really?" said Maddox. He looked at D'Arcy, who looked blank, and said, "Casey."

"Oh," said D'Arcy.

"What time was it, Mr. Dangerfield?"

"Oh, about eight-thirty. He got all the money out of the cash register and he took a whole case of Bourbon too. I called in right away—"

"Suppose you take Mr. Dangerfield down to have a look at Casey," said Maddox. "It could be we've already got him, Mr. Dangerfield."

"Well, that's quick work," said Dangerfield mildly.

D'Arcy took him away, and Maddox brooded over that tablet for ten minutes and then got up and went out. Whatever little message was trying to get through to him hadn't worked its way out of his subconscious yet, and he wished to God it would; he had the feeling it might be important. Until he climbed into the Maserati he hadn't any clear idea of where he wanted to go, but as he switched on the ignition he decided, and went up to Fountain and turned right. Forty blocks east, he turned down Hillhurst and presently slowed to turn into the parking lot of the Sunnyvale Convalescent Home.

As he waited for the chance, Mrs. Cleveland came out of a side entrance, her tall graceful figure and straight carriage unmistakable. It was sprinkling very slightly and she had a pixie-like transparent rain hat over her dark pompadour, was wearing a shocking-pink raincoat. Maddox pulled the Maserati gently into the curb. She got into a new bright green Pacer and pulled it around the lot in one sweep to the exit drive, its left-turn blinker on. Maddox waited until she'd pulled out into a break in traffic, turned into the lot and around to the exit, and had to wait awhile to make a left turn himself; but the green Pacer was only a block ahead, and he kept an eye on it. Separated by half a dozen cars, they proceeded down Hillhurst to where it turned into Virgil, and down that to Wilshire. A little break in the traffic showed him the Pacer's right-turn signal blinking; he switched on his own, and slid over into that lane, only two cars behind her now. And he didn't know why he was doing this, except that it struck him as a little unusual for the efficient Mrs. Cleveland to leave her job in the middle of the day to go—where? For all he knew it might not be unusual at all, but he had the idea that head nurses of well-run convalescent homes were supposed to be at their desks during working hours.

The Pacer went on down Wilshire, quite a way, into Westwood, and its right-turn signal clicked on again and it turned into a large parking lot.

"Well, do tell," said Maddox to himself. The building belonging to the parking lot was the elegant new brick and glass building where Dr. Colby Brokaw had his office.

Which, of course, said exactly nothing. There'd be something like a hundred and fifty other tenants there, offices belonging to all sorts of people. He turned in too, but before he had parked she had left the Pacer and crossed to a side entrance of the building. By the time he got to the rank of elevators in the lobby, two were stationary and the other two slowly descending. There was no guessing where she had gone.

He surveyed the board of tenants speculatively: doctors, dentists, optometrists, lawyers, interior decorators, one floor of investment advisers; a dealer in coins; one in prostheses; a private detective agency; a dealer in fine antique jewelry. More doctors and lawyers than anything else, but what did that say? Nothing at all.

And come to think, as head nurse at that place he supposed she could take some time off for private business when she wanted to.

Private business?

Talk about wasted time, he thought. Peasmarsh had his case tied up. He hadn't heard yet about the slur on Aunt Helen's evidence, but he had enough without it. But Maddox didn't like loose ends left dangling, and the one funny little thing was still worrying him.

Just why in hell the switch in names?

He went back to the Maserati and drove up through Hollywood to the Sunnyvale Convalescent Home. No visiting hours, anyone welcome to come at any time: fine. He went in, and down to the wing where Aunt Helen had briefly been. The two nurses remembered him, and gave him rather reserved looks.

"I just want to be sure I've got all the facts straight," he told them, the stupid cop looking guileless. "About Mrs. Vickers, you know." They were annoyed to have routine interrupted, for questions already answered, but he had them rout all the aides on duty again. Mrs. Vickers had been checked in here on the eighteenth, and was here up to last Monday? Yes, yes. It was all in the records; they had to keep records on everything. Paper work, thought Maddox.

He appraised them swiftly and marked out the youngest aide: Ada Wagner. She was staying in the background, not saying much, and her round brown eyes looked wary. She wasn't pretty or plain, just a thin girl about twenty, her dark hair pinned back severely, her blue uniform neat.

He thanked them humbly and wandered out. It was two-fifty. He thought these places probably operated on hospital hours, three shifts: this shift might be off at three, then. He sat in the Maserati and waited. About five past three, women began to drift out, get into cars, and drive off. The Wagner girl came out about five minutes later, walking quickly, head bent against the rain. He got out of the Maserati and followed her up the lot to the staff parking slots, to an old Ford. "Miss Wagner."

She started violently and dropped her keys. "I thought—you'd gone," she said.

"Get in the car—it's raining," he said, smiling at her. She unlocked the door and got in. He followed her into the front seat and shut the door.

"What—what do you want?"

"Just a little bit of truth," said Maddox easily. "I don't think any of you expected the police to be coming around, did you?"

"Well, no. It's not very nice—I never had anything to do with the police before. And I don't understand what it's all about. But if you mean I tell lies, well, I never." He offered her a cigarette and she said she didn't smoke.

"This is a good place to work, is it?" Maddox was deliberately laying out whatever charm he possessed: that peculiar quality, whatever it was, that attracted the females. She relaxed a very little.

"Yes, it is. I mean, if you don't mind the kind of work, and I don't. I like helping people and taking care of them. I mean, it can be awfully hard work, but I kind of enjoy it."

"Mrs. Cleveland pretty strict with the help?"

"No, not very," she said in a colorless tone. "I mean, there have to be a lot of rules in a good rest home."

"And the pay's all right?"

"Yes. What do you *want?*" For once the charm wasn't reaching a female; she gave him one brief, almost panicky look.

"What I said—the truth," said Maddox in a suddenly hard voice. "This is a police case, Miss Wagner, and there's going to be a trial at the end of it. All of you might be called to testify in court." Which was conceivably true, if Peasmarsh decided to fight for one of his witnesses. She went white, staring at him. "Now, that old lady—Mrs. Vickers—she wasn't here all that time, was she? Mrs. Cleveland just told you to say she was. What reason did she give?"

She said faintly, "I—I— We all told you—"

"Yes, you did, and it was a damned lie. Would you testify to that—under oath—in court?"

"Oh, dear heaven," she said. "She never said court—I never did any such thing before. I didn't mean to do anything wrong—I didn't like it, but—but—"

"So suppose you tell the truth now."

She drew a long breath; she was staring straight over the steering wheel, blindly, into the rain. "Oh, dear heaven. You know about it. She never said police either. I—none of us liked it when it turned out to be police. But—and I don't know anything *about* it, I mean what was behind it. None of us do."

"Tell me what you do know."

"Well—like you said"—her voice was miserable—"she wasn't here. At all. That old lady. I—we'd never seen her be-

fore. Mrs. Cleveland got me and Mrs. Wood and Mrs. Emlyn
and Heather in her office—she was in an awful hurry—and
said she'd explain it all later but this patient was coming in
right away and probably there'd be relatives coming right
away too and if they asked we were supposed to say she'd
been there all along, about ten days. We couldn't make it out,
nothing like that had ever happened before, but we didn't
have much time to think about it or talk, because this man
brought the patient in—"

"Describe him for me?"

"He was—he had a foreign accent. Sort of German—a
young blond man, sort of. He carried this woman right into
the lobby and we got her in a wheelchair and took her back to
a room—Mrs. Cleveland had moved another patient so she
was the only one in it. She was unconscious, I thought maybe
she'd had a stroke. And she was in an awful state, she was just
filthy, and nothing but rags on her— Mrs. Cleveland stood
over us while we got her all cleaned up— And then those
other people came with you and took her away. That's all."

"Not quite. What did Mrs. Cleveland tell you afterward?"

"She—she got us and some of the other staff together—that
day and the next day," said Ada unhappily. "She said there'd
been a—an unfortunate mistake, that patient had been in another home that wasn't so—you know, as good as this—and
her relatives were mad, suspected something wrong—and
there might be a lot of trouble if they knew the truth, because
the other place, well, some of the same people owned it that
own Sunnyvale, and we might all lose our jobs. And so long as
the patient was all right now, it was better just to keep quiet.
We—we didn't know—there were police mixed into it—until
you came back and said who you were."

"I see," said Maddox. A mixture of what César had guessed;
and that had been a good tale to feed them. In between per-
suasion and threat. He was feeling very curious about what
hold Parks had on Cleveland. "We'd like you to come in and
make a formal statement about this."

She uttered a yelp of dismap. "Do I have to?"

"We'd prefer it."

"I'll get fired," she said. "Mrs. Cleveland's—fair, but she's
strict all right."

"You might get fired anyway," said Maddox. "Wilcox Street Police Station. When's your day off?"

"Tomorrow." She was feeling resentful now, at having had it dragged out of her, but she was too scared of the police not to come in. "All right," she said dully.

"Ask for Mrs. Maddox. You won't mind talking to a nice policewoman," said Maddox, and ducked out of the car into the rain. She hadn't started the engine when he turned out of the lot.

What the connection was between Parks and Cleveland he'd be damned if he could see. And all that told them nothing they hadn't guessed, and nothing at all about that annoying little loose end—the changed I.D. bracelets.

It was raining harder. He drove back to Wilcox Street thinking, and not noticing the amber at Gower until too late, nearly got the Maserati squashed by a large furniture truck. As he came in, Feinman and D'Arcy were talking to Whitwell on the desk, and Daisy came briskly past on her way to the locker room with a paper cup, a bottle of aspirin, and a box of Band-Aids.

"What's up?" asked Maddox absently.

"I hope you've got a beefsteak in the refrigerator," said Daisy tartly. "Your wife just ran into a thug, she's covered with bruises, and she's going to have a beautiful black eye."

"What?" said Maddox.

Feinman had just spotted him and came over. "Say, I'm sorry," he said, "but I wasn't expecting it. She'll be O.K., and anyway we seem to have wrapped one up."

Sue and Feinman had gone back to L.A.C.C. for Blackwell. This time they brought him back to the station; the atmosphere, said Sue, might be more conducive. The detective office upstairs at Wilcox Street, like the rest of the building, was old and shabby and very utilitarian; and possibly it retained in its very walls some secret aura of all the sordid, bloody, vicious, petty, ugly crimes it had recorded and the people who had done them and suffered from them. At any rate, Blackwell didn't seem to like it much. He looked at them uneasily, and they began to ask him the same questions all over again, and he gave the same answers, and after a while he began to get mad.

"This is just crazy. Do you think if we go over it a dozen times I'm going to tell you something different the thirteenth?" That was exactly what they hoped. "Pauline was my girl—I'd never hurt her—I didn't hurt her. I don't know why you think I did."

"She left that house with somebody she trusted, you know," said Feinman. "You're one of the few people she'd have gone with, that time of night."

"But I wasn't there."

"And she didn't mean to be gone long," said Sue, "because she didn't put on her coat. It was still in the house. She was with someone she trusted—and he never gave her a chance. We've had the autopsy report now, and we know just what happened to her."

He just sat, head bent, as if he didn't hear.

"She was a nice girl, wasn't she, Bill?" said Feinman in his soft voice. "You loved her, you said. Only you didn't want to marry her."

"I—not right away. Not until I could—take real care—till it could be right. That's right."

"Or maybe not ever," said Sue. "And she kept arguing at you about it."

"Whoever killed her," said Feinman, "never gave her a chance, like I said, Bill. You know one of the things we always look for in a case like this is fingernail scrapings—if she fought back, got a little skin or blood off the killer. And she had nice long fingernails, but there wasn't anything there. She never had time to fight back, try to get away from him. Whoever did it just took her by the throat, and he was big and strong enough that she died in about a minute, strangled, just like you'd wring a bird's neck—"

"And then she was dumped up on that hill," said Sue, "just to lie there in the rain for four days. Do you still say you loved her? Nobody who—"

"Oh, for Christ's sake *stop it!*" he shouted suddenly. He was dead white and shaking. "Do you think I haven't thought about it—thought about it—who, when who in *hell* did it—

how? Yes, I loved her—I guess I don't go around showing feelings much, but Pauline—Pauline—" He raised one hand and covered his eyes in a gesture more eloquent than the painful words. "Haven't I *thought* about it? Haven't I— By God, if ever I get my hands on— But who? Who in hell? And now you going on at *me*—as if—as if I could—ever—have hurt her any way—" His shoulders hunched over farther.

Feinman and Sue looked at each other. Quite suddenly, neither of them was as sure as they had been about Bill Blackwell. There was silence in the office for a full minute.

He said in a muffled voice, "Can I go now?"

"Yes, that's all right," said Feinman.

"Just a minute," said Sue, and went to get the sterling sanddollar necklace from her desk. "Have you ever seen this before?"

Bill looked at it. "I've seen ones like it—you see them around." His tone was completely incurious. "On girls and men too. I don't think it looks right, a guy wear jewelry like that. Jim's got one of those, he wears it a lot—and other kinds." He picked up his old trench coat and went quietly out; his feet sounded uncertain on the stairs.

"Well," said Sue. "Jim Warden? That loudmouth swinger? It's silly, Joe. She didn't like him."

"Maybe he liked her," said Feinman. "Let's go and ask him."

It was getting on toward four o'clock; classes would be over at the college. They went up to Harold Way in Feinman's car, on the chance that Warden was home. Feinman eyed the plaque on the door and said, "Very funny."

"I gather the mother must be the same type," said Sue. Feinman pushed the bell and after a minute the door opened.

"Well, hello again," said Warden to Sue. He was natty in brown slacks, open-necked shirt. "How nice to have company on a gloomy afternoon. I was just about to have a li'l old drink, cheer myself up—won't you good people join me?"

"No, thanks," said Feinman shortly. "Does this happen to be yours by any chance?" He held out the necklace, flat on his palm. "We found it in Pauline's pocket."

For one long moment Warden stared at it. When he looked up, the sweat had sprung out on his forehead and his voice was numb. He said, "My God, I forgot she had it—" And then his eyes went wild and he lunged between them, hitting out at random, plunging for the stairs. He caught Feinman off balance; Sue, knocked hard against the wall by his fist, made a grab for him as Feinman sprawled, and was dragged over the top step to roll all the way down, ungracefully. Feinman was up and down the stairs in five seconds, his gun out. He caught Warden at the door, spun him around, and backhanded him, and reached for the cuffs.

But by then the fight was all out of him; he just stared at the cuffs. He seemed to be in a trance when Feinman put him into the car and went back to see if Sue was alive.

"At least," said Sue with dignity from the cot in the locker room, "it was only Joe—respectable married man—who got a look at my underwear. I never realized before how very expressive that British phrase is, arse over tip."

"Don't be vulgar," said Maddox.

"I must have hit every step on the way down, and my eye—"

"Is going to look like an Italian sunset," said Daisy, "and everybody'll think Ivor did it. Court adjourned early—I wish I made as much as those judges for a five-hour day—and I'd just landed back here when Joe brought Sue in. I don't think you'll get that skirt mended, Sue, you put your heel right through it—and you're going to have some lovely black and blue spots, a real treat for Ivor. How's the head?"

"Better, thanks. Of course I'm all right, Ivor—don't fuss. But it was such a surprise—Jim Warden—and I must say I'm dying of curiosity to know—"

"Well, you're in no state to sit in on the questioning," said Maddox. "Why lady cops can't stay in the office and do the paper work all nice and quiet— You'd better go home. Lie down. If you feel up to it I'll take you out to dinner later."

"Of course I feel up to it. It's tomorrow I'm going to be really feeling the bruises."

"You'd better let Daisy take you home."

"All right, all right. Wouldn't you know, I'd just put on new stockings this morning." Sue groaned slightly as she sat up. "Is my eye showing much, Daisy?"

"You can try a piece of steak, but it's going to be a sight to behold," said Daisy cheerfully. "Come on, let's get you home."

They sat Jim Warden down in one of the hard wooden chairs between Maddox' desk and D'Arcy's, and Feinman read him his rights. "Do you understand that?"

Warden nodded once.

"All right, would you like to tell us how your necklace got into Pauline Strange's pocket?"

Warden was staring straight ahead, not looking at any of them. His weakly handsome face was impassive, and then the mobile mouth twisted and he said, almost conversationally, "What a damn stupid thing to do. I just don't stop to think, as my dear mama's always saying. If I'd just said, I never saw it before, what could you have done about it?"

"But you didn't," said Maddox. "How did it get into Pauline's pocket, Warden?"

"Because," said Warden rather viciously, "these goddamn little bitches of females always have to play both ends against the middle. That goddamn goody-goody cheat. They always go for old Jim, the chicks, I practically have to fight 'em off, so it wasn't any surprise to me—that night we're all out on that damn boring date—my chick Patty and Billy boy go to get the pizzas—this Pauline makes with the eyes at me and says she's got a great idea about us. Says would I pul-ease do her a great big favor. Sure I would. I'm always doing favors for the chicks. I figure maybe she's read Billy boy for the deadly square he is and wants to swing a little. I give her my phone number, she asks." They'd taken the cuffs off him now; he got out a cigarette and lit it. "You read me?"

"We read you," said D'Arcy. "That was Wednesday night."

"Yeah. She was a square too," said Warden. "Li'l baby chick had to be home by midnight. But times, that kind don't stay that way. Then she calls me—that next day—I'd just got home. Says, meet her at her place eleven-fifteen—all girly and coaxy she was, she'd be home alone, her dad and mom out, and we could talk. Talk! I thought she'd fallen for old Jim the charmer, and then what she had in mind—" He laughed. "She wanted to make Billy boy jealous!"

"Oh," said Maddox softly. "I see."

Warden's fixed, rather ghastly little grin didn't change. "She was watching for my car—came out and got in. She just knew I'd be nice and pul-ease do her this great big favor, make like I've really fallen for her, and she's never looked at another boy but Billy and it'll make him real mad, he'll want to marry her right away. Says, give her something, my necklace, she can show it and tell Billy I gave it to her—she was a cute chick, and right then I thought it was funny—I gave it to her."

"And?" said Feinman.

"I'd been on a li'l trip that night—I got some speed from a guy I know—few drinks too, I seem to remember. I was a little high, just a little high. I took hold of her and says we put in a little practice, make Billy boy real jealous. But that she wasn't having, oh, no, the square little chicks all alike, don't touch. I never had many girls turn me down, you'd think I was going to rape her, way she squealed—one minute she's all cozy and giggly, it's a deal, Jimmy—and next minute she's don't you dare do that to me—" He looked up slowly. "And next minute she was dead. I don't believe it, but she's dead. I don't know why. I was mad at her just one minute."

It was the kind of recital they had heard before. They felt a little tired. At least this one wrapped up, and all very conveniently at the end of shift.

Feinman said he'd do the overtime, take him downtown and book him in. Maddox called in to apply for the warrant. At least this one couldn't get called anything but Murder One.

Rowan had come in ten minutes before and been on the phone. As Maddox got up he said, "What was all that? Do any good? We just got a make on that slug. Not from the manager's gun. It's out of an S. and W. .25. If the heist man fires it again somewhere— Oh, and Dangerfield identified Casey as his heist man. Just a little more paper work."

"Big deal," said Maddox. He went home to see how Sue was.

She was, she reassured him, really all right—no permanent damage. Her eye was nearly swollen shut and she was limping a little. They went out to dinner, to Michael's for a change, and he told her what Jim had said.

Sue finished her vodka gimlet, and her eyes were somber.

"And that's exactly the silly little kind of idea Pauline would have had," she said. "Exactly on a par with the idea Bill thought she might have had—scaring them. And that—that weak-sister charmer, who just never stops to think—and on the dope— May I have another drink?"

"I guess you deserve it." He signaled the waitress.

"She was a nice well-brought-up girl—just silly, as a lot of girls are at that age—it's a nice family. It makes you feel apprehensive," said Sue.

"What about?"

"A family. Raising children. You can try the best way you know how, but— Lord, some of the parents I've talked to lately, those kids—"

"Just have to have faith," said Maddox.

There was, on Saturday morning, only one item on the night-watch report: Juanita. Again. She'd taken a john for a hundred bucks outside the Blue Echo bar on Santa Monica. Donaldson and Brougham were rather amused by Juanita; Maddox wasn't.

There was a telex from the chief of police in Dallas: an extradition order coming through for Billy Lee Hodgkins, alias Williams.

The phone company had, last night, supplied a list of addresses that matched those phone numbers. They were all over the place.

It was raining. Feinman was off and Rodriguez back. They'd hardly come on shift when a call came in—"Some doctor at Hollywood Presbyterian reporting an attempted homicide," relayed Whitwell. Rodriguez and D'Arcy went to see what that was.

Ten minutes later Peasmarsh called Maddox. He was furious. "She's jumped bail!" he said baldly. "Parks. I never expected she'd try to make bail, but she did—she was released at six-thirty yesterday, and now she's run. I'm here at the place on Vermont. It's cleaned out—we're not sure what might have been here, there should have been a search warrant two days ago—"

"Oh, really," said Maddox. He couldn't say he was unbearably surprised. She wouldn't have had trouble making bail: no record, and not a capital charge. "I don't say it could pay off, but you might have a look at Mrs. Cleveland at the Sunnyvale home on Hillhurst." He explained. It was the first Peasmarsh had heard of that little complication, and he snarled. "Preserve calm," said Maddox. "There's a female coming in to make a statement on it. The implication is that Parks has a hold on Cleveland. But what I'm wondering—"

"All right, we'll see what she has to say," said Peasmarsh shortly.

Maddox looked at the list of addresses. He hadn't been able to persuade Sue to stay home today. He wondered what that attempted homicide would turn out to be. He put the list in his pocket and went out. The rain was coming down harder.

The first address he went to look at, nearest the station, was on Ridgwood Place. It was an old two-story house, long unpainted, fading into the background of old carelessly maintained houses and apartments. He parked, went up, and pushed the bell. After a long time the door opened and a pair of timid brown eyes peered at him.

"¿Qué?"

"I'm looking for Mrs. Parks," said Maddox, friendly. "Is she here?"

"No se." She was young and slim, hugging the door. "Boss lady? Not here." She pointed to her wrist watch. "Maybe here, one clock. Come back, yes?" She shut the door.

The next address was in South Pasadena. It was an ungainly square old three-storied place, a relic, with a chain-link fence around it and a sign on the gate, NO TRESPASSERS. The gate was locked and there was no sign of life about the place except four old cars pulled up in the driveway outside.

They reminded him vaguely of something; for the moment he couldn't think what.

The next address was in Alhambra. It was a big stucco house set back from the street on a big lot: a street that was half business. Maddox parked half a block up, walked back, and pushed the bell.

The door was eventually opened by a slovenly-looking fat

woman in a stained white uniform-dress. "Is Mrs. Parks here?" asked Maddox.

"Sorry, never heard of her. You got the wrong address."

"Are you sure? She gave me this address—"

"No, sir. This is a home for old folks, 's not a private house. No Mrs. Parks, I'm Mrs. Higgins." The door shut finally.

Maddox stood staring at it. A home for old folks. The hair rose on his neck, and quite suddenly the message from his subconscious got through, and he said aloud, "But my God— the government—all the records for the— My God! My God!" He turned and ran for the Maserati. Paper work, the curse of the twentieth century.

CHAPTER 9

"Eleven—" said Peasmarsh, his voice fading.

"That's right. I think. And we'll need a lot of manpower to look. What suddenly occurred to me," said Maddox, "how glibly we said, any other material evidence Parks had got rid of. But the paper work, Peasmarsh, the paper work!— when did she have time? There'd be miles of it, for the government—Medicare, Medicaid—all the itemized statements— and it was just before the first of the month, even if she didn't keep duplicates it would have been there all ready to mail out— And now it looks as if there was eleven times that much—"

"My God!" said Peasmarsh. As an honest and dedicated civil servant, his first reaction was immediate. "Government money! Of course we had assumed it involved embezzlement of federal funds, but as a second charge—my God, if you're right—"

"Yes, we can use the feds. And other forces around. We'd better get on it and look."

"My God!" said Peasmarsh. "Where are you?"

He was a civil servant of unbounded energy. Weekend or no, he and some of his cohorts came out on it; the FBI was activated and, because those addresses were in their territories, the Pasadena, Long Beach, Glendale, and Santa Monica police forces.

They heard enough, just the rest of that Saturday, to give them the general pattern. At the house in Alhambra, the Higgins woman was unexpectedly meek and helpful; it would turn out that she had a pedigree for bad checks, and was nervous of cops. She opened up readily; she'd thought this was all level, a legitimate operation. That place was nearly a carbon copy of the place on Vermont: twenty-two old people, some in wheelchairs, some in bed, mostly vacant-eyed and unresponsive to questions, obviously lacking the tender loving care. There were two employees on the premises, both Mexican girls.

The Higgins woman said sullenly that she did her best. There wasn't much money coming from the church; it wasn't up to her to use any of her pay for food. She'd just been hired to look after the old folks, some church supporting them, and the woman who hired her and paid the bills always saying she had to cut down. Well, the woman's name was Jones. She gave a description vague enough, but conjuring up a picture of Rose Parks.

Peasmarsh and Maddox left six men there and went on with an FBI man, Canotti, to the South Pasadena place. That was a carbon copy too; the woman in charge was a Miss Dooley, honestly bewildered at invasion by the law. There were twenty elderly patients in a deplorable state, two Negro girls as attendants. "Board of Health!" said Miss Dooley, surprised. "I don't know as how anybody could do much better, I only got two hands. They don't pay hardly nothing out, for the old folks, and why the government as has millions can't spend some on the poor old folks—" She'd been hired by a Mrs. Jones, who paid her salary, the bills. Some charity supported the old folks, Mrs. Jones the secretary or something. Well, Mrs. Jones was tall and thin and kind of bucktoothed—Board of Health *and* police, well, what they were up to, bothering honest people—

"Parks!" said Peasmarsh. "Before anything else, we'll have to get court orders, get these people removed, properly taken care of—" But he was gamely energetic, and Maddox was fascinated. They went on to Ridgwood Place in Hollywood. There, a Mrs. Carnaby, three moronic-looking females as attendants, the same story, same description, and nineteen old people, several of them coherent and wildly excited at seeing outsiders, begging to go home, to be listened to, they'd been slapped, starved.

"Parks!" said Peasmarsh in a tone between horror and satisfaction. By then they had loosed a small army to descend on all the other places. The FBI man with them had the gist of the background now and had got interested; they were sitting in the dirty living room of the third place, the rain beating down outside, waiting for phone calls, progress reports. It was five forty-five. "No wonder she ran—when I think of how much government money she must have taken—" He was bulging with righteous indignation.

"Government doesn't have any money," said Maddox. "Only what it mulcts from taxpayers. And it isn't just Parks. It's beautiful, Peasmarsh—a heavenly beautiful scheme, and I just hope we'll find out more about how it was worked, but the main design I can see. No records at any of these places, any more than at Parks' place. And records there'd have to be— miles of the red tape, Peasmarsh, the lovely red tape you bu- reaucrats deal in. The itemized claims on Medicare, Medicaid —they'd been embezzling from the state too, I don't doubt. Itemized claims for every damned little thing, prescriptions, aspirin, Band-Aids, doctors' visits, a whole stack of them for each and every patient—there'd have to be a central clearing house for all that. Parks isn't the mastermind—just a top hired hand in on the cut, but not *our leader*."

"If you ask me," said Canotti, "it'd have taken more than one mastermind to do it all—keep all the paper work straight. And just how that was done I'm not quite clear—"

"Oh, it's beautiful," said Maddox. "It came to me all at once, like a heavenly inspiration, after I'd thought about all the paper work. Because the damned socialistic bureaucracies are so damned finicky about these things—the average dumb citi- zen hasn't enough sense to know what's good for him, so the government has to tell him. All these Medicare accounts re- ceivable, coming from doctors, hospitals, convalescent homes, all those places have to be accredited, regularly inspected, the licenses and accreditation all down in black and white for the computers to pass on. And here's the Sunnyvale Convalescent Home, all open and aboveboard, duly licensed and inspected and high on the list of approved homes. What easier than to set up branches? So the accounts receivable go to Medicare, Medicaid, as from the Sunnyvale home, the computers go to work, it's all duly passed, the bills get paid. There has to be at least one doctor in it too, you know—maybe more—some of those itemized statements have to be authorized by a doctor.

And among the computers and maybe fifty or sixty government clerks making out the checks, who's going to notice that there are about ten times the number of supposed patients at Sunnyvale than it's really got room for? Meanwhile parcel out the actual bodies into these other places, hire as few people as cheaply as possible to keep 'em alive after a fashion. Just names—valid names of people entitled to Medicare."

"I don't know about its being beautiful," said Peasmarsh. "But, by God, those records have got to be somewhere! Even if duplicates weren't kept, it would hardly be just a once-a-month operation—there'd be continuing records, as you say miles of them—I want a search warrant for that home—"

"And Cleveland," said Maddox pleasurably. "Because Cleveland is tied in, all on account of Aunt Helen." He wondered if Ada Wagner had come in to make that statement. He began to laugh. "Oh, Aunt Helen! What a bevy of cats she did let out of the bag, all so innocent! Just because Parks got flustered, taken by surprise—and no wonder, when it'd probably been running as smooth as a Rolls for God knows how long, no trouble. And I'll tell you another thing—"

The phone rang and Peasmarsh snatched it up, listened, and murmured. When he put it down he said, "Another one—Long Beach. Twenty patients. A Mrs. Cobb and staff of two. She tells the same story, only she says Mrs. Jones didn't come to pay her at the first of the month like always, she's out of money to buy groceries, pay the girls."

"O frabjous day," said Maddox, "that's lovely too—of course not—by that time they were anticipating trouble, the police had been fetched in—all on account of dear Aunt Helen—and they were possibly figuring already on cutting their losses. Waiting to see which way the cat jumped, anyway. But I'll say something else, Peasmarsh—"

"Cleveland," said Peasmarsh with a snap of his teeth like a good watchdog. "Of course she's tied in—the business of Mrs. Vickers—the home—and that's the logical place for all those records. I'll have a search warrant in two hours—"

"Maybe it'd be a good idea to get another one," said Maddox. "We don't want to misplace her like Parks. You haven't got any evidence on a federal charge yet, but you can make it intimidation of witnesses to start, and caution the D.A.'s office to hold up the indictment. We don't want her jumping bail too. But damn it, we haven't got her full name for a judge—"

Peasmarsh said precisely, "By God, I'll back that woman into a corner before I'm done with her! I had some of her grand manner just before you called— Her name's Gwendolyn, I noticed it on the checkbook on her desk—"

Maddox yelped pleasedly and Canotti said suddenly, "Jesus H. Christ." He'd been scribbling on the back of an envelope for some minutes. "I'll be goddamned. I've just been figuring what these jokers must have been taking, and I don't believe it. If they had an average of twenty patients at each of these twelve places, and an average take of five hundred per patient per month—my God!"

It was still raining.

All the various activities on it went on fast and furious on Sunday, and on and on: more and more people were coming in on it—four police forces, more FBI men, everybody in Peasmarsh's office. There were something over two hundred patients out of those substandard homes to find new places for somewhere, somehow; they'd all have to be medically examined, questioned where possible. Search warrants were put through for all those places, but that was probably an empty gesture. It was in the cards that some of those women would be charged with mistreating the patients, but this had gone beyond a simple felony charge now; they were talking about a great wad of taxpayers' money filched, and it was going to make headlines when it was wrapped up.

Maddox got home about seven and told Sue about it over warmed-up beef stew. "And I hope to God we get that warrant on Cleveland right quick. Did Ada Wagner come in?"

"She did. I felt rather sorry for her."

"And thank God it was her day off, but she'll be back at work tomorrow. Not a very cunning female, one look at her and Cleveland could guess she's been telling tales. They've all —whoever the rest of them are—got away with a hell of a lot of loot, and I'd hate to see her take off and vanish into the wild blue yonder."

"The attempted homicide," said Sue, "is something offbeat. A whole family poisoned, the doctor thinks, and he can't figure out how. Just an ordinary family, all living together. Their name's Hunter. Nobody else was in the house."

"Um," said Maddox. Peasmarsh called him at eight o'clock to tell him about two more pseudo-Sunnyvales. At another place in Long Beach they had found twenty-seven old people, most of them senile, crowded together in unspeakable conditions in a six-room house, under the supervision of a single female who'd been dead drunk when they forced their way in.

Belatedly Maddox called Rodriguez and told him about it; the manpower at Wilcox Street would be getting deflected off routine business on this; though the main charges would be federal, it was a mixed bag of police responsibility. Rodriguez, who even more than Maddox appreciated the offbeat ones, said *"Es hermoso sin pero—*beautiful with no buts. One of those sweeping grand designs, you don't really appreciate the artistry till you study it a little. *Dios,* when I think what they might have taken over a period of time—"

"Yes, and we don't know how long it's been going on. What I'm fussing about is Cleveland. I'd take a bet she told Parks to run, you know. She must—"

"'Take the cash and let the credit go.'"

"Must have realized there's more investigation going on. Only one thing comforts me, in a way."

"What could that be?"

"The magnificent way," said Maddox, "she met the little crisis of Aunt Helen. Not only at the time, but when you and I came along and leaned on her, she sat there cool as be damned, ready to spit in anybody's eye, and told us that whopper—her and her records—without turning a hair. She's a gambler, César, and it could be she's decided to face it out, take the chance we can't come up with enough evidence."

Peasmarsh called him at ten to tell him that court orders were coming through, and a sixth place was being examined now; it looked just the same. Twenty minutes after he'd hung up, he called again to say that the warrant on Cleveland had arrived. "I'm still here at the FBI office. But that charge is technically out of your office, and Canotti says—"

"Yes, we'll be on it," said Maddox. "Bright and early."

He and Sue and Rodriguez went out at eight-thirty to the Sunnyvale home, wondering if she'd be there on a Sunday. She wasn't. The receptionist, a different one, looked at them doubtfully when they asked for Mrs. Cleveland's home address. "What—what's the matter? What do the police want with Mrs. Cleveland?"

"You'll probably be hearing, but it's too long a story," said Maddox. "Give. You must know where to reach her in an emergency."

She wrote it out for them in silence; Maddox passed it to Rodriguez with one lifted brow. Cabrillo Drive in Beverly Hills. They were in Rodriguez' car, to have room to bring her back.

It was a new block of garden condominiums, set about with balconies, manicured landscaping, colored floodlights at frequent intervals, an enormous pool in the central patio. "Not a dime less than a hundred grand," said Rodriguez in the lobby, "and maybe more." The carpet felt a foot thick. It was all deathly quiet, very private; only money could buy this seclusion.

She had one of the top units. Even the elevator was silent. They walked down to the end of the hall and Maddox pushed the bell. Unhurriedly, presently, she opened the door. When she saw them her usual cool, remote expression didn't change; only her eyes went blank for a moment. She didn't speak.

"We have a warrant for your arrest, Mrs. Cleveland," said Maddox formally. "And there'll be some more people coming with a search warrant for your apartment."

"May I ask what the charge is?" she said evenly.

"Only for openers, intimidation of witnesses." Maddox smiled at her. "We didn't want you running away like Mrs. Parks. As soon as we locate all the records and trace the loot, it'll be a federal charge—embezzlement. The feds don't fool around with plea bargaining or reduced sentences. It'll work out to a fifteen to twenty."

"Not without any evidence," she said.

"Oh, they'll be coming up with that. All your branches are

getting closed down now," said Rodriguez, "and we'll just wait for more government checks to show up."

She gave him a contemptuous smile, turned and walked into the room, sat down, and lit a cigarette. "I really don't know what you're talking about, but I suppose I can't argue with a warrant."

It was an elegant and very expensive place, the living room twenty feet square, furnished in French fruitwood and gilt: from the white shag carpet to the crystal chandelier it shouted *money*. Maddox regarded her where she perched on the arm of the sofa, her excellent figure showing to advantage in severe black hostess pajamas. He didn't think those particular government checks would be showing up in the regular mail delivered to the Sunnyvale home, and apparently neither did she.

"I think we'll wait," he said. "The feds won't be far behind us."

She shrugged.

The feds, three of them, arrived ten minutes later with the other warrant. They left Sue sitting with her in the living room and went through the place systematically. It was quite a place. She hadn't been able to resist enjoying some of the loot in private; it was doubtful that she socialized any with the staff at Sunnyvale, to have them speculate about it. There were closets full of expensive clothes, a lot of expensive jewelry in velvet boxes in dresser drawers, expensive cosmetics in the bathroom. There was also obvious evidence of a male presence, but probably—they agreed—as an off and on thing. One side of the closet in the second bedroom held a man's silk dressing gown, nylon pajamas, good if anonymous sports clothes—slacks, shirts. There was a little pile of men's underwear in a bureau there; two pairs of men's shoes. one pair of leather slippers, on the closet floor; an electric razor in the medicine cabinet.

There didn't seem to be a scrap of paper in the place. Certainly there weren't any bulky medical records, case histories.

They came back to the living room. "What about your husband, Mrs. Cleveland?" asked Rodriguez.

"I divorced him ten years ago," she said.

"And who's the gentleman who sometimes shares this place with you?"

"I really think that's my business, isn't it? Aren't you supposed to read me all about my rights? And I suppose I'm allowed to pack a bag."

Maddox nodded at Sue, who accompanied her to the bedroom. When they came out she'd changed to a smart navy and white dress, carried a velveteen coat, a navy bag, an overnight bag.

"We'll be going over that home," said one of the feds. They walked out quietly.

All the way downtown she was silent, but none of them had the feeling she was afraid, or even angry, or defiant. She seemed largely indifferent. They booked her into the jail; she had only a little cash with her, cosmetics, clothes; the clerk confiscated a nail file and handed it all back. She walked off with the matron without a backward look at them.

"Ivor, those clothes!" said Sue. "I'd bet not less than twenty thousand just for what's in her closet."

"I bet. Let's wait for NCIC." The prints had gone out, and in fifteen minutes the telex came back: no want. Her prints weren't known anywhere, she was clean. "Just like Parks," said Maddox. "Well, for a first caper they picked a big one, didn't they?"

For the next four days the thing expanded. Peasmarsh and his team had the worst job in a way, dealing with all those people, though Wilcox Street lent a hand at all the interviews. In all, the eleven pseudo-Sunnyvales had contained two hundred and twenty-six people, and those coherent enough to be questioned had to be. Because at least one part of the tangle was still a mystery, there was a lot of unraveling to be done.

The feds had descended on the Sunnyvale home in anticipation, which shortly faded. The offices and nurses' stations were a mine of records, but they were all the records of the actual patients at the home. There was uproar and dismay among the staff.

"They've got to be somewhere," said Peasmarsh, annoyed.

"Sure they're somewhere," said one of the feds. "We don't know how many people were in on this, but there had to be at least one doctor. Maybe more. Maybe the dude she was shacked up with. There are a lot of places to look."

"Six or seven doctors coming here, seeing patients regularly," said another, "by the records. Could be one or all of them. There'd be too big a stack to fit in a lockbox, and they'd have to have them handy, to make up the receipts every month. But we'll be looking at the banks too."

In the interviews with the patients, of course there emerged the common denominator: they were all old people with no one in the world to check up on them, care about them. They had all, at one time or another, emerged from hospitals into the substandard rest homes, most but not all from the General —from other hospitals all over the county. Now they were all in various hospitals again, for medical examination. A rather surprising number of them—those who were not senile—were found to be capable of looking after themselves. They'd been regularly fed the tranquilizers: captives solely because they were eligible for the Medicare.

And monotonously all those women, from all those places, repeated the same story: they'd just been taking orders from Mrs. Jones. Paid to look after the old people. She came and handed out the pills, medicine the old people had to have; paid them in cash, paid the rent for the houses, the bills. All of the women were poorly educated and of small intelligence, incapable of getting or holding anything but domestic jobs. They'd been hired in various ways, from employment agencies, from ads in the papers. It was obvious that some of those places had been in existence before others; the women had held the jobs three years, two years, four years, three years: a couple of them said they'd replaced others fired by Mrs. Jones. The girls they'd hired, or she had hired, to help them with the old people were of the same general type.

And there was nothing, no evidence at all, to link Gwendolyn to that operation. But the mere size of the operation— there had to be another mastermind than Rose Parks.

They would, of course, go on digging. In a case like this the feds wouldn't give up easily. As well as everything else, now they had the names of those patients, and whether Gwendolyn and company had kept duplicate records or not, the bureaucracy loved the red tape and hung on tenaciously to the miles of it. The Medicare bureaucrats were looking back to find out just how much had been paid out, to whom, for what, under all those names. And there were a lot of banks to look at. Money had to go somewhere, and when it was in the form of paper it had to pass through banks. The feds had the big guns to look at bank records very thoroughly.

"This is a hassle," said D'Arcy on the following Friday, looking harassed. "Everything piling up here while we get roped in on the feds' business. Nobody minding the store. I wish you'd take a look at this homicide, Ivor. Joe and I can't make head or tail of it."

"Somebody said, attempted."

"That was when it first showed up last Saturday—the day you had the inspiration and blew it all up into a federal case. The father died on Sunday. Sue and Joe and I've been doing some work on it when we could, and there's just no evidence to suggest anything. Come back home and look over the local crime scene for a change, will you?"

Maddox supposed they ought to. Most of the hectic part of the federal case was over: the old people taken care of, search warrants executed. The feds were quietly going about their business on it, digging for evidence, and it was just to be hoped eventually they'd come up with enough to link Cleveland in good and tight, and locate everybody else in on it.

He looked at the reports on the homicide without much interest at first, but the very shapelessness of the thing intrigued him after a while, and he passed them on one by one to Rodriguez at the next desk; nobody had had any days off this week. The Hunter family—John J. Senior, Hildegarde, and three grown children, Anne, Adele, and John Junior—all lived together in the family home up on Outpost Drive. A week ago Thursday they had all been taken violently ill after an ordinary dinner at home, prepared by Mrs. Hunter. The family doctor had been called, Dr. James Wilberforce, and had sent them all to the hospital. Puzzled by the fact that they'd all been taken ill at once, he had ordered various tests, and on Saturday morning the results had come in: they'd all been poisoned with arsenic. As, fortunately, the house had been shut up since and no cleaning up done, he was able to run tests on the leftover food. This was on Monday, after the police had been called in and John Senior had died. The arsenic had been in the lasagna, which had constituted the main dish; specifically, it had been in the grated Parmesan cheese added to the lasagna.

"Which, I thought at the time, would be easy enough to do," said Sue. "The lab says it was a common rodent poison, fine white powder. And grated cheese—well, I know all the gourmets say it ought to be grated fresh every time, but who does? When you can get it already in a can with a shaker top." She was looking quite like herself again; for a few days her eye had been surrounded with an interesting variety of colors, but the swelling had gone down and the bruises were fading—like the other bruises. "And that was the kind they used. Quite easy to twist the top and pour in the rat poison."

The autopsy on John Senior had just come in. The rest of them were out of danger now, and all back home again. They all said bewilderedly that they couldn't think of anyone who'd want to do them any harm. "Of course we've been looking around, when we had time," said Feinman, "but there's just nothing."

"I've tried to tell you a little about it, but you've been wrapped up in Gwendolyn," said Sue. "I don't suppose you really listened. Hunter had quite a lot of money, but he'd worked for it—both he and his wife. He inherited a little, and started out with one market—it's now expanded to a chain of thirteen. He still managed it all, he and the son. Everybody we talked to said he was a very fair, honest man—everybody liked him—no grudges, no threats, no union trouble."

"Oh, yes?" said Maddox.

"Nobody was at the house that afternoon. Mama and the girls were there alone. Papa and Junior came in about six after a day of market managing—there was an office downtown—and they sat down to dinner about six-thirty. And the grated cheese was all right when they had spaghetti the night before, and nobody but the family had been in the house since."

"Oh," said Maddox. "Loving family?"

Sue's nose wrinkled thoughtfully. "Well, nuances. Papa was boss in his own house, but they all seem to have been fond of him. And when it was aimed at all of them—you can see how funny it looks, Ivor."

It did, but they seemed to have asked all the indicated questions on it and looked in the appropriate places without turning up anything suggestive.

There'd been three more heist jobs. Somebody had flown in from Dallas with that extradition order and taken Billy Lee Hodgkins off their hands.

Nothing new had been heard of Juanita. There'd been an autopsy on Peter Berry, and the slug in him had been fired from Margaret Peller's gun, so that was that. He wondered if D'Arcy had been making any progress with Joan Berry. He wouldn't have had much time this week.

"I'll brood over it and see if anything comes to me," he told Sue.

"You do that."

And there had been a couple of cautious stories in the papers already: the FBI investigating suspected Medicare fraud. Thinking lazily about the funny homicide, Maddox drove over to the Atwater district after lunch.

He found Aunt Helen in the back yard of the little house on LaClede Street, leaning on a cane and talking to Myra Foster. It had stopped raining on Monday and all week had been bright and clear: this was a beautiful day. The fat black cat Sammy was stalking a bird, but not as if he really meant anything by it. "We were just talking about what I might take with me," Aunt Helen told Maddox. "Things that might grow back East."

"You're getting along without the walker, I see."

"Oh, just fine." She cocked her head at him pertly. "Did you come to ask that?"

"Did you happen to see something in the paper about a Medicare fraud?"

"No—why?"

"I just thought you'd like to know," said Maddox, "that you're the one uncovered it. If you hadn't happened to trip over Sammy, and end up in the wrong place—"

"You don't mean it!" said Myra Foster. "You mean that woman was—for heaven's sake!"

"The feds are roaring all over looking at bank records and questioning people, and we've rescued over two hundred poor old people from involuntary servitude, and in the end we hope there'll be quite a few people in jail—"

"All because of Aunt Helen." Myra started to laugh.

"And because you came hurrying across the country to locate her," said Maddox. "Something to be said for having a family."

On Saturday morning there was a conference called at FBI headquarters downtown. Maddox and Rodriguez sat in on it, a lieutenant from Specialized Divisions at L.A.P.D. headquarters, and a rabbity little man who was the chief of the regional Medicare bureau, and Peasmarsh and one of his cohorts. Half a dozen feds made up the party.

The master of ceremonies was the local FBI chief, a big gray-haired fellow named Spaulding. "We thought you'd all better be brought up to date on this thing—in case any of you locals have any bright ideas, we'd welcome them." He had a sheaf of papers in front of him at the long conference table. "I want to correlate all we have for you, and then tell you where we stand. First of all, this was a very, very cute operation, gentlemen. Very cute all the way. We've sorted out the M.O. with a lot of looking and thinking, and we've tied in the Cleveland woman good and tight—but so far that's all.

"This is how it was set up. The Sunnyvale Convalescent Home is owned by a corporation, a perfectly honest outfit that owns several of these places. All the financial records goes to their own accounting office, and everything at that end is perfectly kosher. What Mrs. Cleveland did was to set up a second account in the Sunnyvale name. The regular bank account for the corporation is with the Bank of America. She hasn't any access to that, of course—all the money going out and coming in is in the hands of the board of directors. She set up the other one at Security Pacific, nearly five years ago. It looks just as kosher, on the surface, the checks deposited, the checks against it cashed. Apparently for the overhead—rental of building, utility bills, maintenance, employees' wages. There's a whole list of dummy employees and nonexistent businesses —that's how they got hold of the loot. Supposed payments for hospital supplies, doctors' visits, all sorts of payments. All dummy recipients. We've got handwriting experts examining the endorsements on those checks—literally hundreds of them —but so far as they tell us anything up to now, it looks as if only about four or five people did the endorsing. I don't have to tell any of you how easy it is to get the kind of I.D. most businesses ask for cashing checks."

"Walk in and apply for the driver's license," said Maddox. "John Jones, nonexistent address. Credit cards, a dime a dozen. Just ask."

"That's right. Practically all the supposed salary checks were cashed at supermarkets. The bigger checks were deposited in dummy business accounts—hospital supply houses, pharmacies—and mostly came right out again, in cash. There are seven banks involved so far. I said it was a cute operation. It must have taken them a hell of a lot of their time just passing the checks—it could be they had some help on that. We don't know yet. It's pretty clear that it was the Parks woman who took care of setting up the phony convalescent homes, hiring the help and paying them. The story was that the old people weren't entitled to any help from welfare, a church organization was supporting them—" Spaulding snorted. "My God, of course leeches like this, you couldn't expect them to have an ounce of Christian charity, but all those women were told to keep expenses down, there wasn't much money. None of them were the kind of women with enough sense or education to realize that any indigent elderly people are entitled to Medicare. It could be, some other women hired that way did have the sense, asked questions, and got fired.

"There was a mail drop for the incoming checks—a postoffice box at the Hollywood station, in the name of the Sunnyvale home. That wasn't covered up so well, but it was unavoidable, you can see—government checks addressed that way. Now don't anybody swear—" Spaulding sat back and brought out a fat cigar. "As to the figures, the best we can come up with is that these—these leeches have taken Uncle Sam for somewhere around a hundred and thirty thousand a month for the last five years."

"Disgraceful!" said Peasmarsh loudly.

"For God's sake, that much?" said the lieutenant from head-quarters incredulously.

"Figure it. An average of two hundred and twenty Medi-care patients, with the expenses running about five hundred a month per patient. It's a hell of a lot of money," said Spauld-ing, "and we can only pinpoint where a little of it has gone. They were keeping the overhead down as low as possible, but even so that added up. Rents on those places, salaries, grocer-ies, utility bills, and so on were running them about thirty-eight thousand a month. Drop in the bucket, when you think of the profit they were taking. Parks had an account at Security Pacific, by the way—a checking account with eleven thousand in it. She cleared it of all but a thousand the day be-fore she was arrested."

"And she'd have a hell of a lot more than that stashed away in a lockbox under another name," said one of the other feds.

"You are so right. Quite a lot of the loot ended up in Cleveland's checking account—cash deposits—but she'll have more stashed away too, where we can't find it. But as far as we can figure out," said Spaulding, "the lion's share of it is just gone. And there's absolutely no link anywhere to anybody else, and we know there was somebody else—probably several somebodies—in it. At least one doctor—"

"And a link, or links, at the hospitals," said Maddox. "There had to be somebody to pick and choose the old people, which ones didn't have anyone to check up on them, were fair game."

"No hint," said Spaulding. "The closest we can pin it down, the hospital offices were informed on the phone—old Mr. or Mrs. or Miss Jones to be transferred to a rest home today, am-bulance there at ten A.M. No known ambulance service made those runs—they all keep records, and we've checked them all."

"So, add in one private ambulance and at least two attend-ants," said Rodriguez. "But with that percentage of profit, why not?"

"But those damn medical records," said the lieutenant, "have got to be somewhere, damn it!"

"Oh, pardon me, gentlemen," said the rabbity man, "but of

course they were. The—ah—originals. I was able to locate all of them for Mr. Spaulding, though it was quite a time-consuming job—"

"Those records," said Spaulding, and sighed. "Yes. Well, let's just say that it was a cute operation. As you know, Medicare statements have to be authorized by a licensed physician. Just as the convalescent homes are required by law to have doctors see the patients at stated intervals, and so many R.N.'s on the staff, and so on. There were seven physicians visiting the Sunnyvale home regularly, and we looked at them first. They—er—all put up a howl, but we looked at them thoroughly. This was before we got hold of the originals of the Medicare accounts. And they're all absolutely clean. Then Mr. White handed us the original statements, and we found that every one of them was signed by one physician. Dr. Jonas L. Greenspan. So we went looking for Dr. Greenspan—we combed the medical directories and medical school records for him. And after quite a while we found him. He got his M.D. from the medical college at U.C.L.A. in 1965, and some time later he entered the army medical corps. He was a ranking captain by 1971, and he was killed in Vietnam." Spaulding sat back and spread his hands flat on the desk. "So that's where we are, gentlemen."

"Oh, that's very cute," said Maddox. "You haven't got any line on whoever Cleveland was shacked up with?"

"Nothing. People in that condo mind their own business. Nobody ever noticed him coming or going. She's keeping her mouth well shut, and why shouldn't she? She's got a bundle put safely away, and whether she's madly in love with him or not, fetching him in—and I agree, he's probably the principal —would just put her farther out on a limb. As it is, she sits still and hopes we can't get quite enough evidence to add up to a long sentence. And I guess that's it."

"Damn it," said Maddox, "there must be something to spot —to add up to something." He thought about that homicide; sometimes, of course, there just wasn't.

"Like what?" asked the fed Canotti. They were standing in the corridor outside the conference room.

"That condo," said Rodriguez meditatively. "It was their private place, you know, Ivor."

"We took it apart looking," said Canotti.

"I see what you mean, César," said Maddox. "The place they let down their hair. Oh, they were careful—just in case—but they'd had such a long run, everything going so smooth. Damn it, I say there's got to be something there, at least to suggest a direction."

"Look, we were through everything," said Canotti. "The clothes. He's about six feet, medium build, size ten shoe. What the hell does that say?"

"I'd like," said Maddox, "to look at it again."

"I never heard the L.A.P.D. uses ESP," said Canotti. "What the hell, I've got nothing to do the next couple of hours but work on bricks without straw."

They went up to that elegant condo, in Canotti's car. Looking around it, Maddox didn't wonder whether she'd ever contrasted her surroundings with those of her hapless victims, because as a cop he knew something about human nature. It would never have crossed her mind.

He also knew, as a cop, how to search a place; as did Rodriguez. And everywhere they looked, Canotti said in a bored voice, "We've been through that."

There was nothing. The address book on the little gilt desk where the phone sat held the only paper in the place, and all the addresses and numbers had been checked, all innocuous: hairdresser, drugstore, service companies, garage; she didn't seem to have any personal friends at all.

Maddox stood in the middle of the bedroom, frustrated. And yet he felt there had to be something here. Gwendolyn and the mastermind—an unholy alliance you could say—but this had been the place they could relax, let down their hair. Completely at random, he moved over to the dressing table and opened the top of a big, square, gold jewel box.

"We looked there," said Canotti. "Just costume stuff."

There was a tray that lifted out. Under it was a jumble of earrings and brooches, and one small scrap of paper: a sales receipt from Bullocks', crumpled. "We saw that," said Canotti.

Maddox fished it out and flattened it on the table. There was another smaller scrap of paper folded tightly inside it, probably by accident hidden. "What's that?" asked Canotti, and came to see.

It was a receipt for a fur coat in summer storage, at a furrier's in Beverly Hills. "I'll be damned if I know how we missed that," said Canotti. "Let's go have a look. You never know when something'll turn up from the smallest lead."

At the furrier's, an exquisitely blond clerk took the receipt and drifted away, to drift back with the fur coat in a plastic bag. "That'll be forty dollars plus tax, sir."

"We just want to look at it," said Maddox. "What is it, by the way?"

The attendant gave him a shocked look. "Why, it's a Rubin exclusive, sir. Very rare snow leopard. It's worth at least ten thousand dollars." She looked from one to the other of them. "Excuse me, I don't know that I should let you take it if— even when you have Mrs. Cleveland's receipt—I'd better call the manager."

They showed badges to the manager, who was shocked at police on the premises. "So, who's Rubin?" asked Rodriguez.

"Georgi Rubin, sir, a very well-known fur designer. Really I don't understand—"

"We'll give you a receipt for it," said Maddox. "Is he in business around here?"

"Six blocks up Wilshire," said the manager, "but I really don't understand—"

They drove up there and found the shop, discreetly tiny, discreetly lighted, thick carpet and walls of mirrors, and asked for Rubin.

He came to them from the back, a jaunty, portly little man with mournful eyes; and before he asked what they wanted, one hand reached to touch the soft fur over Maddox' arm. "Police," he said to the badge, and looked anxious. "How can I help you?"

"This coat, Mr. Rubin—we were told you made it. Can you tell us anything about it?"

"But of course I can tell you. A good fur, it is nearly as individual as a fingerprint, sir. Besides, this is indeed my design, and in each of my designs is a private number. This is a very fine fur, very rare. I have handled, perhaps, only forty—fifty— in twenty-five years."

"Is that so?" Rodriguez was interested. "Then you could tell us who bought it originally?"

"Certainly, it will be in my records. Of course it is possible that the original owner had resold it—"

"Just look up who bought it," said Canotti.

"I will look." He went away, and ten minutes later came back with a slip of paper. "It was a doctor, gentleman—I remember the name when I see it. He bought it for his wife. A Dr. Colby Brokaw."

CHAPTER 10

Canotti called Spaulding, who came out in a hurry. "He won't have office hours on a Saturday," said Canotti. "There's a home address on Loma Vista in Beverly Hills."

"So let's go," said Spaulding grimly.

It was a long, low red-brick house with half an acre of trimmed ivy around it, and cars in the circular drive. Canotti parked in front and they walked up the curving drive and pushed the bell. Almost at once the door was opened by a uniformed maid, whose mouth fell open as she stared at the four badges proffered.

"Is Dr. Brokaw here?"

She said faintly, "P-police? There's a luncheon party—" There was a long hall running down from the front door, giving on a large patio with a glimpse of a sparkling bright pool. Closer at hand was talk and laughter from a crowd of people. "Yes—you want to see the doctor?"

"Yes, please," said Spaulding. With one backward look she scurried off.

It was a large, open-roomed house. There were little knots of well-dressed people to right and left, in big rooms either side of the door. They stood waiting.

He came sauntering up the hall to them casually, glass in hand; for whatever reason the maid hadn't said *police* to him and he was totally unwarned.

"Dr. Brokaw," said Spaulding, and held out the badge. "FBI. We'd like you to come downtown to answer some questions."

Brokaw stood rigid, looking at them, the little smile on his face fading. His long thin mouth flattened under the nobly-arched nose. "Indeed," he said in a thin voice. "Questions about what, may I ask?"

"About some substantial embezzlement from the federal government," said Spaulding, "and your relations with Mrs. Gwendolyn Cleveland and Mrs. Rose Parks."

He set his glass down very carefully on a table in the entrance hall. "I have a house full of guests. I suppose this couldn't be deferred."

"No, sir. You're coming now."

He nodded. "Just let me have a word with my wife, please." He didn't make any trouble. He came back in a minute or two, got a hat and coat out of the front closet, and came to them. But they didn't hear any answers from him. It was after one o'clock; they took him downtown and left him to sit and worry awhile while they had lunch, and came back and tackled him, but he sat mute and only opened his mouth once.

"I wish to see my attorney," he said.

"But this has got to be it," said Spaulding. "We'll have search warrants in an hour—this has got to be the jackpot. And thanks very much for the break, Maddox."

"Just luck. We'd be interested in what turns up."

"We'll be in touch."

But Maddox didn't hear from Spaulding until Sunday morning, when he called the office at a quarter to nine. "You might as well come down to sit in on this," he said. "It turns out to be your business too, they've been taking the city for welfare in most of those names. Oh, it's all turned up—my God, has it turned up, with vengeance! Yes, we've got all the medical records. There was a great big stack of them in cardboard cartons in a closet in his office. This month's accounts receivable on the way to being made up."

"Congratulations," said Maddox.

"We haven't had a word out of him yet, but we've arrested his office nurse and the other two he hired—not that they're any more nurses than I am, those two. I thought L.A.P.D. ought to hear."

"Thanks so much—I'll be right down."

The mountainously fat office nurse was Dorothy Willoughby; she really was a nurse, and she had a good deal to say for herself, resentfully and loudly. She sat overflowing the chair in Spaulding's office, all three chins quivering with defiance. She said she'd worked for the doctor nearly twenty years, since he'd been in practice. "And if the government's bound to give all that money away, I don't see how anybody can be blamed for taking it," she said forthrightly. "God knows the doctor did enough charity work he never got paid for. And it wasn't all that easy a job, either—hours and hours of paper work to do, and all on top of the regular work on the doctor's files."

"You and Mrs. Cleveland did all that?" asked Spaulding.

She wasn't feeling reticent, knowing it was all over and nothing to be gained by silence. "That's right, with the Parks woman. Whatever we took we earned, you wouldn't believe the work it was."

"It was the doctor, of course," said Maddox, "who picked out the patients. Seeing the case histories, able to spot the ones without any family to take notice of what happened to them." She nodded sulkily. "And then how did it go? Can we guess—with seven different clerks at the General hospital, other hospitals, in addition to all their other chores checking the convalescent homes, which had space for how many—you, or one of the other girls in the office, would call and say it's been arranged for Mrs. Smith to be transferred to the Sunnyvale home tomorrow at ten A.M., an ambulance is ordered. And it was taken for granted that somebody else at the hospital had arranged it. Was that it?"

"That's right," she said shortly.

"And what about the ambulance?" asked Canotti. "That was all arranged too, of course. Expense wasn't really any object, was it? Who drove the ambulance and where did it come from?"

"Oh, if you're bound to know every little whipstitch," she said angrily, "it was my brother and a friend of his. Right at the beginning, doctor asked if I could arrange that, and I did —Ray's always glad to pick up extra money. The doctor bought an old second-hand ambulance, Ray keeps it in his own garage. Whenever there was a new patient, or we had to move an old one, they'd do it."

"Address?" said Spaulding.

"Oh, New York Avenue, La Crescenta. You'd find out easy enough anyway. Your coming down after all this time—we never thought anybody would. Why should anybody care, all that money just for reaching out and taking it, and everything done so careful—" Her chief emotion was resentment, that was clear.

"The mills of the gods," murmured Canotti. "I'll send somebody up to La Crescenta," and he went out.

"And you had to *think* about all that paper work, you know. Plausible-sounding expenses and payments and all—it wasn't easy."

"I don't suppose so," said Spaulding.

"I don't know why you had to come *interfering*," she said; and Canotti looked in briefly.

"Bill's just brought in Mrs. Stapleton," he said.

"Good. I think," said Spaulding to Maddox, "she may have a little of interest to tell us. I guess that's all we need from you now, Miss Willoughby. There'll be a statement for you to sign later."

She heaved herself to her feet as Canotti came to take her arm and said, "And you needn't think I'd have told you a thing if I hadn't seen that you'd found all those records. Snooping behind people's backs!"

After Canotti took her out Maddox laughed, but Spaulding just frowned. "After all I've seen, I still wonder—how do people get that way, Maddox? So damn wrong-headed?"

"Here's Mrs. Stapleton," said Canotti.

Mrs. Jean Stapleton was youngish, rather pretty, and very nervous at being questioned by the FBI. She said readily that she worked for a CPA firm; Dr. Brokaw was one of their clients. She came into his office once or twice a month to work on his books. She kept looking anxiously from Spaulding to Canotti to Maddox. There'd never been any question about it before—and she didn't have anything to do with anything else there, the patients or the medicine or—

"It's nothing like that, Mrs. Stapleton," said Spaulding. "Do you remember being at the office on a Monday—two weeks ago last Monday?"

She thought. "Yes, I was. I'm usually there on a Saturday,

but that week I'd got all behind, I have six or seven of these
outside jobs and— Yes, why?"

"There were some people came to the office—a Mr. and
Mrs. Foster."

"Oh," she said. "Yes. I shouldn't have left the door open. I
told them the office wasn't open, but they wouldn't listen.
They kept demanding to know where some woman was—one
of the doctor's patients. I kept telling them I hadn't anything
to do with the patients, didn't know anything, but they just
went on and on insisting—it was really very annoying, when
I was behind with the work. I thought that woman was going
to have a fit, she was so mad, and finally—it was sheer
desperation—I looked in the doctor's files. But I couldn't find
the name there—I forget what it was—and they kept on and
on, and I sort of rummaged and found a stack of manila
folders in the closet, and the name was there, with an address
scribbled in pencil in one corner—" She looked at them wor-
riedly. "I suppose I hadn't any business going into his files—is
that what this is about? I'm sorry, but I'd never have got rid
of them otherwise."

"No, it's all right," said Spaulding. "We just wanted to know
how it came about. It's quite all right, Mrs. Stapleton, you
didn't do anything wrong."

Maddox was laughing as Canotti ushered her out, and she
gave him a last puzzled look. "Oh, our mighty Myra!" he said.
"And—I'm sorry, Spaulding, but the idea of the innocent Mrs.
Stapleton stumbling across those records when a couple of
weeks later you were hunting them high and low—and not
having a glimmer of what they were—just because Myra was
so insistent—and of course somebody had scribbled the Vermont address there as a reminder where the new captive had
been taken—and when the Fosters saw Brokaw on Saturday
he'd probably genuinely forgotten Aunt Helen's name, one
among many—"

"You've got a peculiar sense of humor," said Spaulding.

They talked to the other two girls Brokaw had employed,
but agreed they were small fry. As Brokaw had told Maddox
before, he wasn't in private practice to any extent; he hadn't
needed two extra office nurses at all, and from what they got
out of those two, their main job had been cashing checks.

"We got right on this yesterday," said Canotti. "We picked those two up last night, and you'll be interested to know that between them they had all sorts of I.D.'s—good ones—for over a hundred different dummy names."

They were neither of them nurses, Joyce Hall and Sally Wilson: just a pair of young women doing a job as directed and not much concerned that it was illegal. The principals in the case were taking enough profit that they could pay the hired help. Even then, all those checks must have kept most of them busy.

Ray Willoughby and his friend were picked up with no trouble, the old ambulance located and towed in for examination. Willoughby was as annoyed and resentful as his sister. "Well, for God's sake, I never thought anybody'd get onto it after all this time! Hell, what did it matter anyways? Government giving away all that money, why the hell shouldn't we take some of it?" Neither he nor his pal, John Brooks, had much of a brain for plots, and they hadn't understood very clearly just how the money was finagled out of the government by way of those old people. They'd just done what they were told to do and taken the loot they were handed with no questions.

On Monday, when both the principals had had time to talk to lawyers, Spaulding had them brought into his office together. He and Canotti, Maddox and Rodriguez, were waiting to see how they'd react.

Gwendolyn Cleveland was brought in first, as elegantly smart as always in a navy suit and white blouse. Her expression was wooden. But a moment later when another fed ushered Brokaw in, it changed. She hadn't known he'd been arrested, that they had got that far. Her mouth went taut and her eyes widened; her hands went out to him and then dropped. She said, "Oh, my God. Oh, my God."

"The world's not at an end," he said. "Just, there it is, Gwen. You know I said last year we ought to get out, and destroy all the paper, and stay out."

"How the *hell*," she said, "did they drop on you? It was all covered up—there wasn't any way they could—"

"Never underestimate the law," said Spaulding cheerfully. The attorneys, aware of the evidence now, would have advised them where they stood, that it would be a waste of time to fight the case.

They looked at each other for a moment, and then she said suddenly, recklessly, "Damn it, darling, it was fun while it lasted, wasn't it?" She walked over to a chair, sat down, and lit a cigarette.

Brokaw sat down in the chair Canotti offered and just waited.

"Would you mind answering just one question, Dr. Brokaw?" said Maddox. "Just as a matter of curiosity—you must have been earning a very respectable income, as an eminently successful surgeon. Why go to all this risk and trouble to take more?"

Brokaw smiled slightly, fingering his arched nose. "Everybody always wants more money, don't they? My wife has expensive tastes, shall we say. And there was Gwen."

"You'd planned to divorce your wife perhaps," asked Spaulding, "and marry Mrs. Cleveland?"

"Oh, no. Why should I? My wife keeps a very pleasant home for me. And Gwen had had quite enough of being tied down to a marriage."

"Damn right," she said shortly.

"How," asked Spaulding, "did you happen to know about Jonas Greenspan?"

He sighed and looked down at his fine surgeon's hands clasped lightly in his lap. "I taught a class in dissection at the U.C.L.A. Medical Center for a couple of years. Greenspan was interning there. I heard later he'd been killed. It was—as good a name as any."

"Where did you get hold of Parks?" Maddox asked her.

Her lip curled a little. "She and I worked together at the General fifteen years ago. I knew she'd be just the one to jump at a deal like this, and she did. And before you ask, no, I haven't any idea where she is. I'm just sorry you couldn't hang on to her too. If anybody deserves to be punished, well, she did most of the real dirty work."

"I'm just curious, Doctor," said Rodriguez. "As a medical man—trained to relieve suffering—didn't it ever cross your mind, bother you a little—all the misery and fear and suffering you were causing all those people?"

He raised his head, and his eyes were cold. "Sentimental," he said. "It's a subject I happen to feel strongly about. People like that are useless to the world—they're the walking dead. I've always felt euthanasia would be the most sensible course for incompetent elderly people, as we use it for animals."

"Is that so?" said Maddox softly. "But as long as there was the hefty profit to take by keeping them alive, you might as well have it as the next man?"

He just shrugged.

The feds would get their case wrapped up; they were still digging up and analyzing evidence, and they were looking for Rose Parks. They had traced her back to the nursing school where she'd trained and found a graduation photograph; an artist had done some work on it, to add twenty years, and the result had been passed out by the thousands to police, security guards, officials at airports and bus terminals and railroad stations. It could turn her up; the chances weren't very good.

Maddox and Rodriguez went back to their own beat that Tuesday.

One of the new heisters had got identified out of records, and there was an A.P.B. out for him. Jim Warden had been indicted. The funny-looking homicide was still up in the air. Rex Slaney would probably come to trial sometime next month, and somebody would have to spend some time in court offering evidence. At least Daisy was back, the narco trial finally concluded.

There had been two more muggings along Sunset on Saturday night, and some massive vandalism to an elementary school. They also had another unidentified D.O.A., found on the street by some people coming out of a late movie. This one really did look like an old drunk who'd died a natural death.

"We'd better shove that homicide into Pending," said Rodriguez after reading Feinman's latest report on it. "There's nowhere else to go."

"I don't like to leave things dangling," said Feinman, "but I suppose you're right. I keep feeling there's got to be a handle to it—it was such a simple thing. I thought I'd turned up something when I came across the row with the neighbor, but it fizzled out."

"What was that?" asked Maddox.

"Oh, the fellow across the street had a row with Hunter—Senior, that is—over leaving his car in the street. That's a damn narrow street, and it meant this neighbor had to back and get his own car out. But it was just an argument, he said he'd just lost his temper, and he likes the rest of the family fine, said he felt sorry for them, the old man what you'd call autocratic."

"I was hoping," said Sue, "that you'd have an inspiration on it, Ivor. A hunch."

"The L.A.P.D.," said Maddox, "isn't supposed to use ESP. There was just one thought I had about that funny homicide, and I don't suppose it's much use."

"What?" asked Sue and Feinman together.

"Well, one thing in the reports—they're not Italian—either Mrs. Hunter isn't a very good planner or they all must have cast-iron digestions. Two rich indigestible meals on successive days—spaghetti, lasagna, and all the indicated trimmings, garlic bread, green onions, ripe olives—"

"Oh, for heaven's sake," said Sue. "If you call that an idea—! I've got to finish this report. I just hope D'Arcy's having a nice time on his day off, he had a date with his new girl."

Just then Sergeant Whitwell sent up a new call: reported child rape and beating, the squad car there now waiting for an ambulance. Maddox and Rodriguez scooped up Sue and went out in a hurry on that.

Feinman sat there thinking. He'd had a queer feeling about that homicide all along; of course it had been a queer case. The nearest he could come to putting a finger on the feeling was that he felt he ought to know more about it than he did. Which didn't make much sense.

Nobody had been back to talk to the Hunters since last week; there hadn't been any reason to. Now he decided that he'd talk to them once more, and if nothing suggestive showed, he'd agree to shove the damned thing in Pending. He drove up to Outpost Drive, that narrow curving street above Hollywood, and parked just down from the old stucco house.

The door was opened by the younger girl, Adele; she was about seventeen, the other one, Anne, a year or two older. She looked flushed and pretty, and he heard laughter from the living room.

"Who is it, dear? Oh—" Mrs. Hunter came forward. "Mr. Feinman. Have you found out anything?"

"Not yet, Mrs. Hunter. I just thought I'd like to talk to you again."

"Well, of course, come in." There were a lot of maps and travel folders spread out in the living room, and the other girl and John Junior, who was a nice-looking young man about twenty-four, were laughing over them. "We're planning a trip to Hawaii," said Mrs. Hunter. "It's quite exciting, we've never been anywhere—oh, dear, that sounds heartless, I know, but —you can't bring people back."

"At least you'll have a little fun for a change," said her son, smiling at her.

Feinman thought the girls both had new dresses on, and more make-up than he'd noticed before. He sat down in a chair and looked at them absently. He really didn't know what new questions to ask them; he really didn't know what he was doing here at all. The only thing that came into his mind, foolishly, was what Maddox had said about the meals.

"Was your husband fond of Italian food?" he asked. She looked surprised.

"Goodness, yes, and Mexican things too. To think," she said, "that I'll never have to face another pan of lasagna again! Or spaghetti, or tamales—"

"Or that horrible garlic bread," said Adele.

"Or salsa— Oh, Mama, how that sounds!" Anne laughed and flushed. "As if we're glad Papa's gone, and of course we're not." She started to help her brother fold up the maps.

"I should hope not, and in such a dreadful way," said her mother. "You see, Mr. Feinman, John had a very hearty appetite and unfortunately he liked a good many things the rest of us don't, but I had to fix them for him every so often. And you can't make just a little spaghetti, there was always some left

over and he disapproved of waste—" She sighed. "And he
disliked it so if I fixed something different for the rest of us—"

"All sit down to a simple meal as one happy family!"
chorused the girls, obviously quoting the late Hunter.

"Girls! That doesn't sound at all nice. How on earth did we
start talking about this? Oh, you asked."

"Well—" said Feinman, and paused. "You told us the lasagna was on the stove, keeping warm, until the men came
home."

"Yes, that's right." She looked a little impatient at being
taken over this again; her gaze wandered to the folded maps.
"I knew they'd be in soon, I'd just been setting the table in the
dining room—"

"And the back door was unlocked," said Feinman.

"Yes, I told you. I suppose somebody could have come in
and— But it's absurd! Not ten steps away, I'd have heard—"

"And then they came home, and you fixed all the last-
minute things, the salad and garlic bread, and you all sat
down to eat."

"That's right."

"Bringing the lasagna in at the last minute."

"Yes, so it was hot. And," she said vaguely, her eyes on the
maps, "we'd no sooner sat down than John was complaining—
I'd forgotten the Parmesan cheese, I hate the stuff so—but
Johnny got up and fetched it from the kitchen."

There was a little silence. "Oh, he did?" said Feinman. He
looked at John Junior, who was suddenly standing very still in
the center of the room.

"Yes, what— Why are you looking like that?" She stared at
Feinman. "What—does that mean? It wasn't—we'd used it
before— Why are you *looking* like that?"

"It's all right, Mama," he said in a steady voice. "It's because he knows that's where the arsenic was, in the grated
cheese. I never really expected I'd get away with it, and I
haven't any business getting away with it." They were all
speechless, watching him. "It was a horrible thing to do. He
wasn't a bad man. Not by his own lights. But just piling all
the money up in the bank, never letting any of us enjoy it a
little bit—never letting you fix the house up even a little,

waste of money—never letting the girls have parties, it'd cost too much—telling me what a damn fool I was to keep saying I hated a good job in a good business I'd inherit, want to fritter my life away on music— And all those years ago, Mama, I know how you scrimped and saved to pay for my piano lessons, and then he said it was all damned nonsense for a boy and made me quit—"

"*Johnny!*" she said in a whisper.

"Well, at least you and the girls are out of it now," he said heavily. "I knew we'd none of us ever get away, out from under him, until he was dead. And that was the—the easiest way I could think of to do it. I knew the rest of us would be all right because we never ate much of that stuff—but the way he'd go at it, gulping it down as if he was starving, two or three plates of it— Well, I thought—that ought to do it." He looked at Feinman with dull curiosity. "I was beginning to think I had got away with it, but I guess it was too good to be true."

Feinman was nearly as surprised as the rest of the family.

Sue said, "If you're developing clairvoyance, it ought to be useful on the occasional mysteries."

"Just talking off the top of my mind," said Maddox. "That was a funny one all the way."

They'd got the formal statement from him without difficulty, and he was booked in jail. "And now the family can spend some of the money on his defense," said Feinman.

"I don't think he'll let them," said Sue seriously. "That was really why he did it, he said—'to rescue Mama and the girls.'"

The heister hadn't been picked up yet. The child rape had turned out to be all too real, and as the child wasn't quite five, they hadn't got any kind of description; they'd be out now talking to neighbors, other kids, for what it might be worth. It had happened in the back yard of a vacant house, and Dabney and Rowan had gone out with the lab truck but hadn't picked up anything useful at all. It was discouraging, because one like that they wanted to drop on quick, before he did it again.

They drifted off at the end of shift. The papers were saying it might rain again. Sue beat Maddox home and was changing her clothes when he came in. "Creamed chipped beef," she said. "Asparagus. Lettuce and tomatoes. Toast or—"

"Baked potatoes."

"We won't eat for an hour. I really must find out more about those microwave ovens."

Down at the station, Brougham and Donaldson came on night watch presently. They didn't have a call until nine-thirty, when there was a heist at a twenty-four-hour dairy store on La Brea. They got a fairly good description of the heister, who was just about as opposite as you could get to the one they already wanted.

They had just got back, tossed a coin for the job, and Brougham had started the report, when there was some scuffling on the stairs and loud voices, and Patrolman Nolan came in with two citizens. He was panting slightly and looking harassed.

"Now, listen, you, calm down and take it easy!"

"I just wanna see you put that li'l cheat in the slammer! You jus' take her—"

"Calm *down!*" said Nolan. "It seems to be a robbery charge, Brougham—I was cruising down Fairfax when I heard shots, and this pair were out in the middle of the street struggling over a gun—" He laid a little Colt .32 on the desk. "He says the girl tried to hold him up—I couldn't make sense out of it or get his name, I thought I'd better bring them both in."

Brougham and Donaldson were staring at the girl. "Juanita!" said Donaldson happily. The description certainly fitted. The girl was a very light-skinned Negro, small and curvacious and skimpily clad in a short black shirt, tight red cardigan, black tights, and knee-high boots. She had a medium-sized Afro hairdo, and her pretty face was much made up with mascara, eye shadow, deep red lipstick. The man was a great big blond fellow, and he was drunk, but still on his feet and looking dangerous.

"It was just outside this bar," said Nolan.

"We can guess," said Brougham.

"Li'l bitch pull a gun on me," said the man, and suddenly

lurched toward her and grabbed her by both shoulders. They wrestled together, Nolan swore and tried to pull him loose, and they all fell in a tangle on the bare floor. Brougham and Donaldson leaped in to halt the fray, and pulled the drunk to his feet roughly.

"My God!" said Nolan. They all looked.

Juanita was getting up slowly. The Afro wig was upside down on the floor, and facing them was a sexless-looking creature with smooth short-cropped black hair, the made-up face below incongruous. It looked back at them for a second and then burst out laughing.

"You gonna put me back in the joint, I reckon you better know which I am, fuzz." White teeth gleamed. "On the surface like, I'm a he." He unbuttoned the cardigan to show an enormously padded brassiere clasped around a flat male chest.

The drunk roared, Nolan swore again, and Brougham and Donaldson began to laugh hysterically.

They thought it was so funny they called all the day-watch men to tell them about it, after they'd sent him to jail.

His name had turned out to be Sam Podmore.

On Friday afternoon the unexpected happened. A sharp-eyed bank guard, retired from the Pasadena force, spotted Rose Parks entering a bank in San Marino. He called the feds, and she was still there, down in the basement where the safety-deposit boxes were, when they arrived. She walked out of the elevator into their waiting arms, and in her new brief case was two hundred thousand dollars in cash.

Spaulding called Maddox to tell him the good news.

"Have you got her there now?" asked Maddox.

"Yes, we're just about to take her downtown. There's not much to talk to her about." Spaulding chuckled. "It's all been said."

"Will you hang on to her there for half an hour, please?" said Maddox. "I've got just one question I want to ask her. After all we've heard and found and surmised, there's one little loose end hanging out that worries me."

"Sure," said Spaulding, surprised and amused. "There's no hurry."

She was sitting in a straight chair beside Spaulding's desk, and looking at her, Maddox thought that a greater contrast to Gwendolyn Cleveland could hardly be imagined. She had on new, better clothes—a green knit dress, smart black shoes, a green hat with a feather—but her figure was graceless and angular, her long bucktoothed face sullen under too much make-up.

She looked at him and said, "You."

"That's right," said Maddox. "I've got just one question for you—no, two, come to think. Mrs.? Have you shed a husband like Mrs. Cleveland?"

She said in a flat voice, "Gwen was one of the lucky ones, pretty. No. People say Mrs., and what's the point telling them they're wrong?"

"I could have told you that," said Spaulding, "from the nursing-school record."

"Will you please tell me," said Maddox, "the one loose end left—why in God's name did you change those I.D. bracelets? On Mrs. Vickers and Miss Runnels? What was the point?"

She looked at him sourly. The game had been played and lost, but she still had some memory of her former power. She said a little scornfully, "I should think you'd have worked that out. The place I ran, we used to put them there awhile at first, so I could see how they'd be—which ones were senile and no trouble, and which'd need the pills to keep them quiet. I was the only R.N. in it beside Gwen and she had her own part of the job to do. Those two came in together, and I had a look at them, and right away I saw the Runnels woman wouldn't last long—a bad heart. The Vickers one was sound as a bell and good for twenty years or more. Gwen said it'd be better just to switch them. You see, there was more to be got out of Runnels —she was daughter to a railroad man and what these unions have got out of the railroads now, she was due his pension, four hundred a month the rest of her life. On top of all the Medicare—"

Maddox drew a long satisfied breath. "Thanks so much," he said.

"And then those people showed up—how could we know she had a family? Nobody ever came to the hospital—"

"Put it down to Nemesis," said Spaulding.

On the way back to the station, on sudden impulse, Maddox got off the freeway at Santa Monica and threaded through narrow streets to La Mirada.

The trailer was gone from the drive of the little house; the lawn was even more beautifully green and trimmed than before. Maddox parked, went up and pushed the bell, and Anton Czerny opened the door. He was clean and neat in work clothes, a nice-looking old man.

"The policeman," he said, and smiled. "The house, all fixed up fine—you see."

Doug Wyler came up behind him. "Well, hello," he said. The little living room was neat and clean, ceilings and walls repaired and painted, a new green carpet on the floor; there was new furniture, bright and modern, and new curtains at the window. There was a good smell from the kitchen.

"I just wondered how everything was going," said Maddox.

"Fine," said Wyler. "You wouldn't believe how fine. Everything all fixed up again. And do you know, after that TV thing, a columnist on the *Herald* did a piece about it, and people started to send him money. You wouldn't believe it. People feeling sorry, sending in five bucks, ten bucks. It's got up to nearly seven thousand bucks. Would you believe it?"

"People," said Maddox, and he said it fondly.

"People," said Wyler. He put his arm around the old man's shoulder.

"It is hard to understand," said Czerny in his careful English. "The bad things happen, maybe to bring the good things. Doug and Linda say, I am to be adopted grandfather." He smiled. "I teach Linda some Czech things to cook."

"That's fine," said Maddox. "Just fine."

As he pulled into the bay opposite the station on Wilcox Place, it began to rain. He climbed the stairs and stood on the landing. D'Arcy and Feinman were typing reports, Ellis cussing as he changed a typewriter ribbon. In the other direction, Daisy Hoffman was typing and Sue brooding over her notebook.

"Don't tell me, we can hear, it's raining again," she said.

H 3

Maddox took the notebook out of her hands, leaned over, and kissed her hard. "Well!" said Sue, startled. "What prompted that?"

"I'll take you out to dinner," said Maddox. "It's nearly end of shift. Somewhere really fancy, just to celebrate. In spite of all we see, love, it could be a worse world. Always more of the good people than the bastards."